# one

love by numbers book five

# one

## love by numbers book five

e.s. carter

emtippettsbookdesigns.com

Cover design by Cover Me Darling and image licensed from Fotolia.

*In dreams and in love there are no impossibilities*

*– Janos Arany*

*To G for being my soul mate and best friend; trust I seek and I find in you.*
*To L, G & A for inspiring me to be better.*
*To P for being the best big brother a girl could ever want.*
*I miss you.*

*To everyone who is missing someone. Remember them with smiles and not tears.*

# Note for the reader

The entire 'Love by Numbers' series, including this book, is set in Britain and has been written using U.K. English. It contains euphemisms and slang words that form part of the British spoken word, which is the basis for this book's writing style.

Please remember that the words are not misspelled, neither are any of the words that use U.K. spellings.

If you would like further explanation, or to discuss the translation or meaning of a particular word, please do not hesitate to contact the author. Contact details can be found at the back of the book.

# prologue

## *Isaac*

The incessant buzz of the tattooist's gun fizzles through my mind, becoming a physical manifestation on my skin in the form of goose bumps.

It's not the mechanics of getting a tattoo that has such a profound effect on me; it's the finality. Choosing to have these words made indelible is what has my mind spinning.

When I walked into 'Blue Door Ink' a shitty looking tattoo parlour on some unknown street in L.A., I had zero intention of doing anything except looking. I hadn't yearned for a tattoo or thought over my plans. I simply walked in because my last shoot had been a bust and the name above the bright blue door was cool. Plus, the burlesque girl behind the counter with a Monroe piercing and full sleeve tattoos made my dick stand to attention in a way nobody had for a long time.

Now I'm lying here, underneath said girl, and not in the way I had first intended.

She's going to mark me.

She's going to use her delicate and elegant hands, fingers tipped with talon red fingernails, to wield a needle dipped in ink across my shoulders and scar my virgin skin.

I'm not thinking about her, though.

When her weapon of choice makes initial contact with my skin and a thousand red ants feel like they are chomping on that one specific point of my epidermis, I think about him.

### Acceptance is Serenity

Not for him.

These words are not for him.

# chapter 1

## *Isaac*

*lick.*

Fine mist settles against smooth, tanned skin in perfect iridescent droplets.

*Click.*

A single bead of moisture engulfs all the smaller ones in its path, growing bigger with every inch of caramel skin it caresses until it pools in the hollow of her neck.

*Click.*

She swallows and that tempting drop of water, an enticing, cool spring well to my parched throat rolls onwards, over the graceful sweep of her clavicle, down, down, down between the small, firm mounds of her bare breasts.

*Click.*

It gathers momentum as it licks over her sternum,

haphazardly following a path dictated by the fine hairs on her silky skin.

*Click.*

I lick my lips, swallowing hard as my thirsty lens tracks each millimetre, capturing the very moment that dewy bead hesitates before it tumbles over the edge and disappears into her belly button.

*Click.*

"I get so turned on during a session with you, Isaac."

I normally find her husky voice attractive, but I'm annoyed that she's moved her position to run her fingers over her breasts and down through the slowly evaporating path of moisture, obliterating the perfection I was still hungering to capture.

"I told you not to move."

My voice is stern, a warning. Céline's ears only hear it as a temptation and her fingers continue to feather across her damp skin, ruining my frames.

"I can't help it, *Mon Amour.* You make me hot and needy. I need you to fill this ache. Scratch my itch."

Her fingers travel further south, slipping under the waistband of the flesh-coloured knickers that barely cover her pussy lips. My eyes flick to the darkening tone of the fabric and the evidence of her arousal. She's wet for me, and my initial annoyance flees with the stirring of my cock.

"Dammit, Céline. Get your fingers off your clit. This shoot isn't over."

I scowl and drop my camera to my side, pushing myself

up from my sprawled position and onto my knees.

"The agency is sending over another model. They want both soft curves and masculine planes. Apparently, sex still sells, and that applies to bottled water too." I give her a disdainful look meant to reprimand.

"So take a break and get make-up to retouch your skin. I want it looking like silk for the next round."

She pouts her plump mouth and brazenly flicks over her clit a few more times trying to provoke a response. I give her nothing but a blank stare, despite my growing erection.

I mean, come on, I'm a hot-blooded man watching a beautiful woman masturbate. I'm only human. I'm also a professional, on set at least. When I'm on the job, I'm all in.

When I'm off the clock, I'll make her pay.

Céline eases from her position with the grace of a feline. She's all soft curves and toned skin. Womanly perfection encased in a beautiful shell. She's also fame-hungry, which makes her a dangerous conquest. In this business, I dare not taint my professional reputation with my desires for sins of the flesh. Not in public, at least.

"I thought you'd be more fun," she huffs as she walks away. Unbothered with her nakedness, she ignores the robe she previously wore into the studio and sways her hips seductively on her way to the dressing room.

She halts at the door, her head turning to look at me over her shoulder. "Let's hope the new guy they're sending is more playful. I'd hate to be left wanting."

She's gone before I can offer a response. Not that I have

one. I'd bite my tongue off before I propositioned her on the job. That doesn't mean she won't be in my bed tonight. I need the release. I feel stretched thin, taut like an archer's bow, stressed to the point of snapping. Losing myself in Céline's body won't fix what's wrong, not that I even know what's wrong with me lately, but it will ease the tension inside me, if only for a little while.

Ever since my brother, Jake, got married I've felt off kilter.

I can't explain it. I mean, I'm happy for him, ecstatically happy, but Jake was the last person I ever thought would get his shit together, and it's left me a little adrift. I'm questioning everything I thought I wanted in my life and coming up short on the answers.

Seconds pass before I realise I'm staring at the empty space where Céline recently stood. I turn myself away from the studio door and make my way over to the set. The lighting needs some adjustments; the softbox needs to add more diffusion, while the honeycombs need to concentrate it on the areas I'm focusing. I should call the tech in to help, but I like my sets closed. I like the control I have when it's just me and my subject.

It's intimate, personal, and my only requirement.

You can't get that same level of connection when others are milling around or gawking. All I want on set is me, my equipment, my camera and something beautiful in front of my lens.

My thoughts stray to less professional activities as I scan through this morning's frames. Shot after shot of smooth, wet skin, and of the sumptuous dips and curves of Céline's tight body.

This shoot is for *Wicked Water,* the premium drink brand that makes billions selling what is most likely tap water, to the aspiring masses. It is my job to convince a significant percentage of those masses that drinking this water will make you as sexy as the beautiful people advertising it.

This morning was all about Céline but this afternoon sees a male model brought into the mix and like the professional I am, I haven't even bothered to check out who he is. All I know is he's due any minute now.

Almost as if my mind has summoned him, the studio door swings open and I feel, rather than see, another male presence in the room. Even as my eyes remain fixed on the screen in front me, I can feel him, and a crushing sense of deja-vu skitters down my spine. I'm frozen, torn between needing to look and wanting to remain oblivious. Don't ask me how I know; maybe it's his smell or just his presence, but I know it's him.

*Him.*

*Flynn Phillips.*

Gorgeous, successful, sinfully hot, and *straight* Flynn Phillips.

The last time I saw him was the night I swallowed his cock, and he roared his appreciation down my throat in hot spurts, before turning over and fucking our third, a model called Evangeline with his still rock hard dick, never sparing me a second glance. Maybe that was the problem; I was the

# one

third, not Evangeline. I was the spare part in a bed made for two. It didn't feel that way, though. For someone who has lived his life not looking for a connection, I was unprepared when my crackling awareness of Flynn Phillips hit me full force. What also hit me, like a sucker punch to the throat was the realisation that this connection was one-sided. His eyes, his body, his entire being, fooled me into thinking he felt this weird vibe between us, or maybe it was my eyes, my body, my entire being that made me the fool. It doesn't matter now, not when he's less than a few feet away from me in *my* studio, *my* space, *my* domain.

All that matters is facing him with my dignity intact and the foolish buzzing in my belly under wraps.

"Hey, Isaac. It's good to see you again, man."

*Fuck.* His voice. The one that's made him millions, along with his ripped body, slides over my skin like a benediction. I'm not a religious man, but that voice makes me want to pray. Pray for strength, pray for weakness, pray for something inexpressible.

Someone listens because I spin to face him with an easy smile on my face and a cheery welcome that sounds authentic, even to my ears.

"Good to see you, Flynn. I'm sorry, I didn't realise you were booked for this gig. I guess I should pay more attention to the brief, hey."

If he knew any of my tells, he would see by the way I run my fingers over and over the ridges on the circumference of my camera lens how off my nerves are. But he doesn't know me at all. My secret is safe, and I lose myself in the comforting texture of the solid grooves against my fingertips and the sight of the sinfully hot man mere feet away.

"It was a last minute thing, my agent called with the offer just yesterday and seeing as I had a spare few days between countries, and I'd heard you were shooting, I thought why the hell not." His deep brown eyes crinkle at the corners with his easy smile, and I daren't let my gaze rove any further than his masculine, yet beautiful face. Flynn Phillips is *all* man. From the tips of his toes to the ends of his unruly, dark brown hair. I want to drink him in from top to bottom. I want to set aside my camera and memorise every inch with just my eyes, sating this weird craving I have whenever he is near. Yes, it's a need that begins in my cock, but it's more than that, *he's* more than that, and the truth of my obsession with him will knock me sideways if I allow it.

"It's good to know you're eager to work with me again." I get the words out, but they feel thick with meaning on my tongue and I drop my eyes and turn my back to Flynn in the hopes he doesn't taste their hidden truth. "I thought a gig like this wouldn't be on your radar anymore. I mean, you're doing good for yourself, Flynn. Real good."

I make myself look busy, collecting up equipment, moving things around the set. I do anything and everything to stop myself looking back at the man behind me.

"Yeah, it's been a wild ride. I never know what country I'm going to be in next and the second book went straight to the top of the charts in over seventy countries. Who'd have thought a lad from a council estate in Bristol would become a jet-setter just from some fitness and cooking videos? It's been a whirlwind, and as much as I've enjoyed every minute, I'd kill for a few months to myself." I can hear him take a seat on the only sofa in the room, but I remain 'busy' enough to avoid looking his way.

"Don't take that the wrong way," he adds when I don't say anything in return. "I'm grateful for the opportunities and loving every second, but isn't it funny how when you get everything you thought you ever wanted, it turns out to not be the thing you wanted after all." His voice has changed from confident to contemplative, and it's enough for me to look at him once more.

He's sat, stretched out across the small sofa, his gaze off somewhere in the distance, allowing me to soak up the view.

Pale grey sports bottoms hang loosely off his narrow hips, a plain white t-shirt stretches taut across his broad and leanly muscled chest, and his skin holds a deeper tan than when we last met. Tied around his wrist is a well-worn leather bracelet that looks handmade, and his feet are clad in his prerequisite sports shoes by the world famous brand with who I know he's just got a huge sponsorship deal.

You see, Flynn Phillips still believes he's an ordinary bloke who once lived in a two-bedroom flat with his factory worker father, stay-at-home mother and older brother, and to a large extent he is, except he was always more than that and now the whole world knows it too.

Flynn, a sports fanatic from an early age, studied health

and fitness in college, and, as a laugh, began posting videos of himself on *Instagram*. His workouts and healthy meal ideas, combined with his boyish charm and ridiculously beautiful face saw him amass over one million followers in a matter of months. Sponsorship, publishing and business deals poured in and just over a year later, Flynn Phillips is an advertising guru's wet dream and the hottest property around.

He's still staring into nothingness a few moments later. Maybe I should say something profound, but I can't get into anything with him again. I'm feeling off as it is, and I can't allow something that happened over a year ago to muddy my head up any further.

"Why don't you head into the dressing room and get Zoey to sort out your bed head and stubble. I'll be calling you back in to shoot in around thirty minutes or so."

His head jerks towards me so fast I think he forgot we were in the same room. He shakes off the slight air of melancholy and replies with a grin, "Hey, this is not bed head, my friend. This," he motions to his thick, dark, wavy hair, "is what my stylist calls, 'Fuckable Couture'. I thought you artsy types all knew the latest trends."

His voice is teasing and his smile genuine, but all I garner from his light-hearted response is 'You *gay* types all like fashion'.

I shouldn't be surprised, I've lived with stereotypes my entire adult life, but I won't take it from a *straight* man whose cock has been so deep down my throat that I can still taste him on my tongue months later.

11

# one

I'm livid and the deep breath I drag into my tight chest does nothing to alleviate the urge I have to use my fists on his too beautiful face.

"Yeah, well, this *artsy type* couldn't give a fuck about the latest trends and doesn't want to hear their model's existential musings about why their glamorous life isn't as amazing as it ought to be. So do us all a favour and get your makeup done so I can wrap this fucking shoot up without acting on my urge to turn your 'Fuckable Couture' into 'Fucked-up Roadkill.'"

My fists clench so tight I can feel my short fingernails breaking into the skin of my palms. I no longer want to pound Flynn into the wall; I want to beat my own head in for losing my cool with this guy when I should've just smiled at his thoughtless quip and not lost my professional cool.

"I meant nothing by…" he tries to explain but I'm done with Flynn Phillips and I need him out of my space.

"Don't apologise. It's been a long day, just…" I motion to the door, "get Zoey to sort you out and let's get today over and done."

I'm such a fucking prick.

Flynn nods once and gets to his feet. His face is a mask of guilt and apology, and I can see he genuinely did not mean his words the way I interpreted them. Maybe I'm the judgemental fool.

I'm such a huge, fucking prick.

I watch as Flynn walks to the door, and just as he touches the handle, I offer my apology.

"Listen, Flynn. I'm sorry for the rant. It wasn't cool and it'd be great for us and the shoot if we could start again."

Without turning back to look at me, he nods once more and leaves the room.

Way to go Iz. Way to fucking go.

# chapter 2

*Flynn*

Why did I come here? Why did I agree to take on this job when I could've used a few days of R and R? I should've taken Elaina up on her offer of a couple of days at the beach. Instead, I got offered a shoot with Isaac Fox, the hottest photographer around right now, and I blew her off. Not a smart decision on my part especially after the last time we met, or rather, the morning after the last time we met.

"You have amazing brows. Do you get them threaded?"

What the fuck is this girl on about?

I mean, she's sweet and cute as a button, but she talks on and on about things I have no idea of, and even when I don't reply she keeps going and going and going. I wonder if it's a nervous thing or if she simply doesn't have an off switch.

I'm about to tell her I have a headache and would

appreciate some quiet before the shoot when the dressing room door swings open and a striking, caramel-skinned goddess strides into the room wearing nothing but a semi-sheer robe that leaves little to the imagination. With her form backlit by the large window that overlooks the bustling street below, I can see every voluptuous curve of her body in high definition.

She stills when she spots me sitting in a chair with Zoey fussing over my face, and a polite but aloof smile takes over her exquisite features. Recognition quickly morphs her pleasant smile into a more calculated façade meant for seduction. I see this look on female faces often. It's one that says 'You're Flynn Phillips, and I'm going to tempt you into my bed.' I'm not going to lie and say that look hasn't been a success for many others, I'm a young hot-blooded, single guy after all, and as I let my eyes rove her delectable frame, it's highly likely it will be a winner yet again. Wasn't I just thinking about getting some much-needed relaxation? What could be more stress relieving than being balls deep inside a beautiful woman?

"Well, hello," she purrs in a heavily accented voice that sounds like it's been dipped in honey. "Aren't you a treat."

Her stride changes into an enticing sashay which only highlights the deep curve of her waist and smooth lines of her hips beneath the diaphanous fabric of her robe. She loosens the belt with deft fingers and allows it to gape a little, generously affording me a clear view of the swell of her breasts.

Zoey huffs under her breath and steps away.

"You need to remove your clothing so I can oil your skin. Iz is expecting you back in the studio in a few moments, so if you could strip off while I grab the…"

The newcomer sidles up alongside Zoey, who is blatantly miffed at being interrupted. "No need, Zoey, my sweet. I can help Flynn get lubed up seeing as we will be all but naked and writhing around on the floor in a few moments time. It will be good for us to become acquainted with each other's bodies before we get in front of the camera. Don't you think, *Mon Cheri?*"

I smile because this girl is good. She hasn't bothered to introduce herself, and her over-confidence should be unappealing, but right now it's a welcome diversion.

I glance at Zoey and thank her for doing my hair and make-up but dismiss her quickly by picking up the bottle of baby oil and sliding it into the French Seductress's hand.

"I think that's a very good idea…?"

She smiles in victory, flashing her pearly white teeth and all but elbowing poor Zoey out of the way.

With feigned embarrassment at not introducing herself, she flickers her impossibly long eyelashes and caresses the bottle between both hands. The look on her face is an attempt at demure while the rhythm of her fingers across the bottle is anything but innocent.

"How rude of me not to give my name," she removes one stroking hand from the bottle and slides it up my bare arm, "I'm Céline Bertrand, body and face of *Wicked Water*.

I wasn't expecting the honour of sharing a campaign with someone as," she flicks her eyes down over my chest to land on my lap before returning them to lock with mine. "*Big* as you. I can't wait to see how explosive this shoot is about to become."

Her blatant innuendo is not lost on me, and I don't bother to fight the grin that takes over my face.

"Well, Miss Bertrand, I can safely say this shoot is becoming more pleasurable by the second. And to think that only moments ago I wished I was on the beach with my best friend. Isn't it funny how situations can improve so quickly?"

I stand and without preamble pull my t-shirt out of the waist of my bottoms before hooking my hand behind my neck to grab the fabric and tug it off in one smooth movement.

I'm not shy about my body. I worked bloody hard to look this good. My business is health and fitness, and I know every inch of my body is sculpted to perfection. That's not me being narcissistic; it's a simple truth. My body is my brand and without it, I'd be lucky to be a minimum wage gym rat right now.

Céline's audible intake of air as I drop my joggers and stand before her in just a tight pair of black boxer trunks is a little over-exaggerated and would usually grate on me, but right now I have a raging hard-on that is eager to come out and play, so I ignore her obvious game playing. Besides, it's hardly a one-sided game. I want to get into her knickers, and she is making it plain that she's more than eager for that to happen.

17

Eyes locked on mine she takes a single step forward and flicks open the cap on the oil bottle. The cool liquid squirts over my chest and drips down my abs to be quickly followed by her nimble fingers and soft palms, but still she keeps her eyes on mine. Just as she is about to oil areas that do not require lubrication, the dressing room door swings wide and Isaac Fox stands in the entryway looking perplexed. His confusion doesn't last long, though, and the look on his face is swiftly replaced by one of fury.

The anger rippling from him charges the air and drags my attention away from the soft touches of the hot woman in front of me. Memories of different hands, *his* hands roaming my skin assault my senses with every second our eyes remain locked. These memories are swiftly followed by a maelstrom of disgust and lust, and I'm not sure which emotion is more prevalent but I grab onto disgust with both hands and force myself to match his angry glare.

*Fuck.*

*Remind me again why I agreed to take this job.*

A small and often ignored voice in my head whispers, "Him." You took this job just to see him.

No. I didn't.

Holding his stare, watching his fists clench and release as they flick from Céline's hands on my slick chest, to my now impassive face, I know I'm a liar. The hard on I sported for the woman in front of me hasn't abated. In fact, I'm harder than I was moments ago, and I know, despite my denial that the man in front of me is the reason why.

True disgust twists my guts. Not at him. At me.

I'm not attracted to this man.

I will never be attracted to this man.

Liar.

Liar.

Liar.

# chapter 3

*Isaac*

*C* *lick.*

Fine mist settles against smooth, tanned skin in perfect iridescent droplets.

*Click.*

A single bead of moisture engulfs all the smaller ones in its path, growing bigger with every inch of firm skin it caresses until it licks a path over his Adam's Apple.

*Click.*

He swallows and that tempting drop of water, an enticing, cool spring well to my parched throat rolls onwards, over the defined muscles of his shoulders, down, down, down over the broad, sculpted mounds of his pecs.

*Click.*

It slows momentum as it deliciously and haphazardly

follows a path dictated by each of his abdominal muscles.

*Click.*

I lick my lips, swallowing hard as my thirsty lens tracks each millimetre, capturing the very moment that dewy bead hesitates before it tumbles over the edge and disappears into the pronounced V that highlights his narrow hips.

*Click.*

I'm so fucking hard it hurts.

I clear the croak in my throat before issuing a new command, "Céline, can you lift your leg a little higher and arch back?"

When she effortlessly moves as instructed and new lines are created on which to focus my lens, I swallow down the churning burn of lust and confusion that bubbles beneath my surface and I get lost in the art of creating something beautiful.

I remove the person that is Flynn Phillips from my head and turn him into a pretty object for my view finder.

He hasn't invaded my thoughts over the last year. He isn't the person that has taken starring roles in my dreams and often my nightmares. Neither did his parting words flay me wide open and remind me of everything I am and everything I'm not.

He's a model behind my lens. Nothing more, nothing less.

If I keep telling myself all of this, it will soon become true because the reality of having Flynn in my space after what happened between us is fucking with my head. I can't allow that to happen. How can one man have such an effect on me?

"Céline, that's perfect, hold that position. Flynn, can you move your arm a little lower so it covers both her breasts?"

Flynn does as I ask, his lips at the curve of Céline's neck where it meets her shoulder, his legs framing her hips as she sprawls against him with her back to his front.

Fuck, they look hot together. Whoever paired them up for this ad campaign was a genius despite the unoriginality of the concept. *Wicked Water* wants a wet, sensual, *hot* series of frames that are sure to come under a lot of scrutiny by the *Advertising Standards Authority*. In fact, I'm sure they are hoping for that to happen. Adverts that push boundaries, while selling a lifestyle choice via the age old, but successful cliché that 'sex sells', always create a buzz. It's my job to make them beautiful enough to also pass as art and not just consumer manipulation.

"Okay, I have enough. Let's do a few of you straddling him, Céline. If you can remove your briefs for this shot, as I need clear lines of your lower back."

Céline doesn't hesitate. She stands gracefully before giving me a sultry smile and shimmying the flesh toned knickers over her hips, down her long smooth legs before stepping out of them and standing bare for both our stares.

Flynn does a quick scan of her body before his eyes return to me. The intensity of his gaze leaves me feeling unbalanced yet unmistakeably turned on. Forgetting my professional demeanour for a moment, I can't help but allow my eyes to follow the plains of his body until they rest on the impressive erection in his tight boxers. An erection that pulses under my stare and forces me to blink away my errant thoughts. When my eyes return to Céline, I can't help but notice the seductive smile on her face or the calculated look in her eyes.

"Shall we, *Mon Amour?*" she purrs, pursing her lips and arching an eyebrow. The question is rhetorical and one she doesn't need a response to, and I know she isn't just referring to continuing the shoot but insinuating something more sinful, more enticing.

I clear my throat and motion for her to situate herself, avoiding any further eye contact by fixing my attention on checking the lighting.

"I'm going to spray you both with some additional mist, so you're gonna get a little wetter, but I'll make it quick."

"Oh, I'm always up for getting wetter." Céline infers in her raspy, accented voice, hitching her hips slightly and eliciting a groan from Flynn as her flesh rubs up against him, a noise that he attempts to cover with a strained laugh.

"I didn't have any idea of what I was getting myself into, did I?" he laughs but the desire in his voice is evident, despite his attempt at keeping this situation professional.

Céline answers by undulating over him once more and my eyes snap to his strong hands as they reach out to still her hips.

"Not the time or the place, I'm afraid." He chastises Céline with a smile in his voice to which she pouts like a child and bats her eyelashes in pretend innocence.

# one

"You guys are no fun. All work and no play…"

Before she can finish the sentence I interrupt, "Gets the job finished and makes the client happy. If you could just channel all the sex you're trying to force into the room into the next set of frames, you guys can both go and work it out of your system in private." My voice is snappy even to my ears, but I've had enough of Céline's games and Flynn's presence. The way I'm reacting today isn't me. I'm the professional but laid-back guy that doesn't get phased by anything or anyone. That's all gone to shit today because I'm barely holding myself together, and I cannot afford to fuck this up.

Thankfully neither of them react to my words and we wrap up the rest of the shoot in under an hour.

*Wicked Water* is going to have an impressive set of images from which to choose. Despite the weird energy I'm expelling, Céline and Flynn nailed the brief, and I have frame after frame of perfection to edit and present.

"That's a wrap, guys. Thanks for today, you're now free to go."

Céline stands and stretches out her naked body. Flynn, ever the gentleman stands behind her and helps her into her robe. Despite not looking directly at them both I can feel they have their eyes on me. It's Céline who speaks first, all innuendo and seduction removed from her voice when she asks, "Want to join us for a bite to eat and some drinks?"

I look up from my monitor and watch as Flynn grabs a towel from shelves and begins to wipe down his wet body.

Distracted by the view I answer, "Thanks for the offer,

but I'm beat. I have to fly out to L.A. tomorrow, so I need to pack."

"I'm sure you have time to squeeze in some food. Come on, Isaac, even you need to relax sometimes, No?"

Before I can refuse once more, Flynn speaks. "You guys should go. I have another meeting this evening but Céline's right, Isaac. Everyone needs to relax."

There are no hidden meanings to his words and the fact he will be absent makes it safe for me to go with Céline. Do I even want to risk going with her? Earlier today it seemed like a good idea to work off some of my stress with a willing partner, but now I'm not so sure. I feel drained. Despite her turning down the tone of her seduction, there's only one way that this will go if I agree and do I want to end up in her bed tonight?

As Flynn pulls up those soft grey sweatpants of his over his firm thighs to rest on his narrow hips, I realise that I do. I want to forget how seeing him again has made me feel, and Céline would be an excellent way to do just that. I turn away from them both as I speak, hoping for an air of casual acceptance.

"Okay, that sounds great. Why don't you go and get changed while I pack away in here? I'll come and get you when I'm done." Then as an afterthought, one that is in no way an afterthought because he's consumed all my thoughts since he walked in here just a few hours ago, I add, "I'll see you around. Flynn. It was great shooting with you again."

Rude I know, but that's all I can offer him without making

it obvious how much seeing him has affected me.

I hear rather than see Flynn and Céline embracing each other and saying murmured goodbyes and then I'm alone.

My shoulders sag with relief and my head hangs low as I collect what's left of my equilibrium.

"I guess I'll see you around."

Flynn's voice is right behind me. I thought he'd left and was concentrating so much on getting my head together I didn't hear him step up behind me.

Trying to cover my surprise I answer without turning around, "Yeah, see you around. Thanks for today."

A warm hand lands on my shoulder, the heat of his skin permeating the thin fabric of my shirt.

"About what happened…" his voice is soft and apologetic.

"Don't, Flynn. It's water under the bridge." My voice cannot hide its air of defeat.

"I was a complete prick, I just… I mean, I didn't…"

I spin around, shaking off his touch.

"I said *don't*. It was a long time ago. Trust me when I say I never thought about it again."

*Liar.*

*Liar.*

*Liar.*

His face is honest, open and… sad.

He doesn't have the right to feel that way. One night and a few hurtful words should never have affected me the way it did.

"I didn't mean what I said."

His eyes hold mine and I swear he's genuinely trying to make amends, but why here and why now?

The answer to that doesn't matter. It's best I shut this down.

"Yeah, you did. You meant every word."

My voice is firm but resigned. Not allowing him to respond further.

He stares at me a beat longer and then nods almost imperceptibly.

"Take care, Isaac. It *was* good to see you again."

And then he's gone without a look back.

Good.

I'm done with looking back.

I know who I am. I'm happy with who I am.

Fuck Flynn Phillips.

# chapter 4

*Flynn*

"Hold the door!"

I have one foot in and one out of the exit when the familiar voice halts me in my tracks, and I spin around to face Céline.

Dressed down in ripped, skinny jeans and a slouchy sweatshirt, she looks nothing like the seductress of earlier and more like the girl next door. Albeit a very attractive girl next door. Natural looks good on her.

"Hey. I thought you were grabbing a bite to eat with Isaac? Did he stand you up?"

She huffs the hair out of her face and lifts a ratty looking sports bag over her shoulder. "No, he's just held up on a call. The agency rang for an update on the shoot so he's meeting me in the bar across the road." I motion for her to exit before me onto the street and she offers me a sweet smile of thanks. Her transformation from the woman who writhed naked on top of me less than an hour ago, into the one now standing before me, is quite a head spin and the look on my face must give my thoughts away.

"I'm just a girl, Flynn. When I'm in front of the camera, I become someone else, an actress if you will. I call it 'escapism', my agent calls it 'method modelling'". She laughs lightly and shakes her head in a self-depreciating manner. "It's a cutthroat business we're in, and I need this more than most, so I do what I have to do to climb to the top."

Huh. Well, she certainly fooled me.

"I have to give you credit, you certainly play the part well."

She places her free hand in the back pocket of her jeans and shrugs, "We're all selling something in this business, are we not?"

"I guess." It's my turn to shrug. "Sometimes the price seems kind of steep, though, don't you think? I mean, how much easier would life be if we could just be free to be who we are without restraints or expectations?"

Her smiling eyes meet mine, and at this moment she's far more attractive to me than she's been all day.

"How about we continue this deep conversation over beer and a burger. I've starved all week for this shoot, and now I just want to sink my teeth into something juicy."

I raise my brows at the tease in her voice, and she quickly backhands me across the chest.

"Get your mind out of the gutter. As hot as you are, I need to refuel. So, are you up for it?"

When I flick my glance from her to the bar across the road, then to the building we've just exited, she nudges me playfully.

"You and the elusive Mr Fox, hey?"

Her comment makes my eyes bug out from my face, and I splutter through my answer. "I'm not sure what you're on about, but I don't bat for Isaac's team."

"And what team is that?" Her voice is light. She's still teasing, but she's aware that she's getting close to the bone.

I force out a laugh to appear unaffected, "The team I'm not on. Isaac's a cool guy and a great photographer, but he's not the flavour I typically go for in the ice-cream parlour, so to speak. I'm a vanilla guy, through and through."

"Huh. I guess I was wrong. Maybe all that sexual tension and testosterone thickening the air in the studio today was a figment of my overactive imagination."

"I guess it was."

"So there's no harm in you joining us then."

It's a statement, not a question and she links her arm through mine without waiting for my response and guides me across the road and into the bar.

It's quiet; the lunch crowd long gone and the evening crowd not due for another hour or so. I head towards the bar to grab a menu and some drinks while Céline snags us a booth in the far corner. Due to the lack of other customers, I get served quickly, and moments later I have beers in hand

and I'm heading over to join her.

"Sorry, I didn't ask what you wanted, but you mentioned a beer earlier so I got two pints, I hope that's okay? If not, I can go back and…"

She grabs the first glass I put down and takes a hefty gulp before wiping the froth from her top lip with the back of her hand when she's done.

"I'm guessing I bought the correct drink?" I smile before sipping the froth from my pint and setting it down onto a cardboard beer mat.

She sighs happily into her beer as if I've just made her day. "I'm an easy girl to please. British beer and a juicy burger and I'm a happy bunny. I guess I'm what I've heard guys call a 'cheap date.'"

When I only offer her my raised eyebrows in response, she laughs before snatching the menu from my hands.

"Don't act so surprised. Just a girl, remember?"

While she reads the menu, I take another sip of my pint and glance out the large windows that run the full wall of the bar, catching the exact moment that Isaac steps out of the doors to his building, phone still in hand. He's distracted by his call and navigating his way across the street, so he's oblivious to his surroundings. It's the first chance I have to really take him in. From the beat-up leather boots on his feet to his jeans that look aged and well-worn, up over his frame to the dark blazer over a plain white t-shirt and a black scarf wrapped loosely around his neck. His face is relaxed and happy as he chats to whoever is on the phone and his dark hair that's almost to his shoulders, whips across his face in the breeze. I've never taken much notice of other men. Sure, I could tell you if someone was classically handsome or not, or if they worked hard on their body, but beyond that, I'd never actually paid any attention. Why would I? I love women. Men are colleagues, workmates or friends, and never has it entered my head to check any of them out. I blink away the thought, unwilling to allow confusion to spoil my perusal of the man who confuses me just by breathing the same air.

He's handsome, even I can see that, with a strong, masculine jawline clad in a couple of day's stubble, and deep-set, dark hazel eyes that are a little bit on the large side for his perfectly proportioned face. Despite his longer hair, he's all man, nothing at all feminine in his looks or his mannerism. I'm thinking all this as if I'm trying to convince myself it's okay to feel this weird vibe between us, but my stomach churns as the word 'attraction' flits through my mind.

I am not attracted to men.

I am not attracted to this man.

It's simply not possible. Besides, I don't even know him.

"*A quoi penses-tu?* A penny for your thoughts?"

Céline's voice breaks my stare at the exact moment Isaac finishes his call and slides his phone into his back pocket before pulling open the door to the bar. He takes a few steps inside, scanning the room for any sign of Céline and his eyes clash with mine as I reply to her question, "I was just thinking that I should maybe go."

Isaac's steps falter and I can see the indecision on his

face. He wasn't expecting me to be here and he's wondering if he should turn around and walk out.

"Don't be silly, you haven't eaten yet and," she looks up to see what has gotten my attention, "besides, Isaac has just arrived. Although I can see you already know that."

I notice the moment he steels himself, knowing that we've both seen his arrival, and walks slowly towards our booth.

My mind is telling me to get up and make my excuses, my body, on the other hand, isn't listening so I drag my eyes away from his approaching form and look down into my pint.

"Looks like I'm interrupting. Three's a crowd and all that, I'll see you guys another time." Isaac's voice cuts through the silence, and it feels as though he's speaking to me, but I can't be sure as I'm still looking at the residual froth on the top of my pint.

"Don't be silly. It's not a private party for two. Come on, I'll scoot over, we haven't even ordered our food yet so you're just in time. What are you having, Flynn?"

I should go. I should really get up and leave.

"Uh, I'll get the steak. This body can never get enough protein."

Why the fuck didn't I just say I was leaving?

"And what an impressive body it is. Hey, maybe you could give me some training tips? I mean, a girl can never have too many tricks up her sleeve." I smile gratefully at Céline for keeping the tone light.

# one

Isaac slides across the seat and sits next to her, his eyes on anything but me. Silence descends across our table once more, making an already awkward situation even more unbearable.

"I'll, uh… go and place our order at the bar if you can let me know what you want?" I risk looking across the wooden surface separating me from Isaac and wish I hadn't when his angry eyes meet mine.

"No. I'll go. I know what you both want, and I'll shout for dinner seeing as you both killed today's shoot. It's the least I can do."

He doesn't bother to wait for a reply from either of us; he's out of the booth and halfway to the bar before I can blink.

"It's funny," Céline whispers, leaning over the table in a conspiratorial way, "I've heard how intense Isaac is to work with, but I was also told that he's a fun, laid-back guy. He's kept that part of himself well hidden today, wouldn't you say?"

"I don't know, I've only worked with him once before. He's a cool guy. Maybe he's just having an off day." I mumble into my pint, my eyes wanting to track the other man to his spot at the bar but my head keeping my focus on the beautiful model in front of me.

Céline looks at me thoughtfully before turning her head to look towards where I know Isaac must be standing.

"Huh. I guess." She looks back at me, a little mischief glinting in her lovely dark brown eyes. "Maybe we should get him drunk, loosen him up a little. God knows, I could do with a fun time."

I stare at her a beat, about to open my mouth in reply when another pint is placed before us both, and I turn to watch as Isaac strides back towards the bar to collect his own.

"I guess he won't be too hard to convince." She chuckles as we both watch him walk back towards us with a pint in each hand for himself, and a barman is walking behind him with a tray full of shots.

"It's been a long day. I figured we could all do with a few drinks."

He turns to Céline as he gets into the booth and it's like a switch has flipped in him. Sitting in front of me now, wearing a smile filled with wicked thoughts is the man I met over a year ago.

The man whose very presence promises things I've never yearned for or wanted.

This is not the uptight man we've been working with all afternoon. This is Isaac Fox.

Charming, engaging and practically dripping with an aura that makes you want to know him.

Makes you want to know all about him.

His thoughts, his dreams, his wants, and his desires.

This man is dangerous to me.

He's everything I've never wanted.

He makes me *need* to hate him.

He makes me *hate* to need him.

# chapter 5

*Isaac*

I got off the phone with the *Wicked Water* rep and quickly shut down the studio. Zoey, the makeup artist who freelances for me on occasion, and Matt the lighting tech, had left as soon as the models were out of the building and they knew I had no more use for them.

I refuse to let myself think about the day because every time I do, all I think about is him. Flynn Phillips.

I'm pissed off with myself for being unable to keep a hold on my weird emotions around him, and I'm thankful it didn't ruin the entire gig, which was a real possibility.

As I begin to turn off the main lights and lock up the studio's front door, the low notes of a familiar ringtone makes me smile.

I've assigned everyone in my family their own personal

tune, all very obvious and very cheesy. Nate, my eldest brother, got '*In Da Club*' by *50 Cent* because he owned so many nightclubs. Jake, who indulged in casual sex even more than I, got '*Womanizer*' by *Britney Spears,* although to be fair, I should change that now seeing as he's happily married to Emma. But the ringtone blaring from my phone right now is '*Loser*' *by* Beck. It might seem a little mean to assign this to Josh, who is two years older than me, but there is a reason, well there are a few reasons.

One, he played this song over and over when we were teens and two, we teased him relentlessly about being a geek who fell in love with the first girl to smile at him and then marry her right out of university.

Therefore, 'Loser' stuck. Although, he's far from one. He's blissfully content, teaches in the same school as his wife and has an adorable little girl called Ivy with another baby on the way. He's more put together than the rest of us combined, well, he was the *only* one of us with his shit together for a long time, but it seems all the Fox brothers are settling down now, except me.

"Hey, Josh. How's it hanging? To the left or to the right?"

This is the greeting I always give him. Again, something that started when we were kids and he would roll his eyes at me, so it stuck. He still rolls his eyes, so it's worth sounding like a moron.

True to form he replies, "One day, you're going to surprise me and answer the phone like a grown man."

"And why would I do that when you always react. It's too

much fun."

He huffs, then laughs, "I'm an adult, Iz. I find it hard not to react. It's a hazard of being around kids all day, and I expect other *grown-ups* to act like adults too, although, I should know better when it comes to you."

"Okay, Daddy Josh, I'll try and behave long enough for you to tell me why I'm being honoured with a call from you. Have I missed some family thing? I know I've not been around a lot lately. Work is manic…"

He cuts me off, "No, you haven't missed anything. Just calling to invite you over this Sunday. Everyone is coming. We figured, what with the nice weather that's forecast, it'd be good to catch up and put on a barbeque. Plus, Laura is on maternity leave from Friday, so it's kind of a pre-baby party."

"Mum and Dad coming?"

"No. They are on their cruise. Three weeks around the Caribbean?" he words it like a question. "We all chipped in for their anniversary, you must remember."

I lock up and step out onto the street before replying, "Oh, yeah. I can vaguely remember sending money to Liam for something. I didn't realise that was now. I guess I should call in more often, seeing as I'm supposed to still live at home."

"Yeah, it wouldn't hurt, but Mum knows what you're like and how much you travel. It just means that you have the house to yourself for the next three weeks. Which, thinking about it, should I be warning you about parties and stuff?"

I can't help the laugh that bursts from my mouth, "No,

*Daddy Josh.* I'm a little on the old side to be inviting the neighbourhood around for parties and turning the house into a den of iniquity, don't you think?"

At that, he chuckles, "Yeah, well, I can never be too sure with you."

I'm just about to step into the bar that Céline said to meet her at when Josh wraps up the call with a, "I've gotta go, the buzzer just rang for next lessons. See you on Sunday, come over anytime, and you're in charge of dessert."

"Dessert?" I ask in confusion because he never normally makes me bring anything, but I don't get a reply because he's already hung up.

"Great." I smile to myself as I swing open the door, "Guess I'm bringing dessert." I slip my phone into my pocket and scan the interior for Céline. The place is reasonably quiet, a handful of patrons at the bar and a few couples sat at the low tables. I continue my search to the booths that line the perimeter and my next breath stutters in my chest when my eyes lock with Flynn's deep brown ones.

*What the fuck is he doing here?*

My legs lock in place, and I can feel the relaxed smile I wore when chatting to Josh, slip from my face. Céline turns to see what has got his attention and when she sees me I know I have no choice but to walk towards them.

My brain tumbles and churns as I take measured steps in their direction, all the while trying to think of a good enough excuse that will allow me to spin around and walk straight back out of here. When I step up to their table, all rational thoughts leave my head as soon as his eyes drop from mine and I spit out some sarcastic remark about three being a crowd. Against my better judgment, I allow Céline to talk me into staying and as soon as I possibly can I'm high-tailing it to the bar to order drinks and food. The last thing my stomach wants is to eat but I place our orders and down a double shot of tequila in the time it takes the barman to pour another couple of pints.

"Hey, can I get a couple more shots to go with these?"

"Sure you can", the young man in front of me smiles, his gaze attentive, open and inviting. He's handsome and has a young, college student vibe, but he does nothing for me or my tumultuous emotions. As cute as he is, if he got down on his knees and offered to drain away all my stress with his pretty mouth, I'd turn him down. Even with my back to Flynn, I can feel him, feel his eyes on me, and I know I'll need quite a few of the shots the guy in front of me is pouring, to cope with even breathing the same air as him.

"Cheers, man. Can you bring them over to my table? I kinda got my hands full." I motion to the beers in my hand and give him a flirty smile, it's not intentional, it's just my fall-back persona for dealing with anyone.

He blatantly scans me from head to toe before he replies, "Happy to help you in any way I can."

This would usually be my cue to offer up ways in which I'd enjoy his help, but I've already turned my back on him to make my way towards our table. I briskly deposit the first two pints in front of Céline and Flynn, before rushing back for my drinks.

The shots are lined up on the barman's tray as he steps around the bar and follows me on my return trip. I swear I hear him mumble 'Nice arse' from behind me and it's just the ego boost I need to shake off some of the nerves that Flynn evokes in me. I cast off the unsure, hesitant demeanour that's blanketed me all day and bring my usual, 'Take me or leave me, but you'll want to take me' persona to the forefront.

As I slide into the booth alongside Céline, Flynn's eyes feel like laser beams across my skin and just knowing that I have his attention invigorates my resolve. Turning to thank the barman for his eager help, I smile up at the young man as he places the tray on our table and with a wink say, "I'll come back and see you if I need any more help."

He leans back and stuffs both hands into the back pockets of his jeans, his stance purposely attempting to draw my attention to his physique.

"You do that." He smiles at me, never once bothering to look at anyone else before turning and with a lazy, confident gait, he walks back towards the bar.

All I want to do is look at Flynn. I want to see his reaction to the young barman's obvious interest in me, but I don't. I fake my mutual fascination and watch the young man make his way back to his other customers, offering him an enticing smile when he looks back at me to check he still has my attention.

He doesn't. The man sitting directly opposite me has it all, but it would be dangerous and foolish of me to make that apparent.

"I think you have a new fan." Céline points out breaking the silence surrounding the three of us.

I don't give her a verbal response. Instead, I pick up a shot and bring it to my mouth. In one smooth movement, I knock it back and savour the heat sliding down my throat and warming my belly.

"Drink up." I motion to the tray of shots. "It's no fun drinking on your own. Playmates are always required for all the exciting things in life."

"*Santé!*" Céline gestures with her shot glass before swallowing down the amber liquid in one large gulp and then wiping her mouth with the back of her hand.

We both raise our eyes to our third; the person sat opposite us who has been strangely mute since I arrived.

Flynn looks from both of us to the tray of drinks, shakes his head, almost like he's clearing away doubt, and then selects a glass.

With his eyes fully on mine, he raises his glass in mock salute and says, "To fun with friends," before knocking back its contents and chasing it down with a gulp of his pint.

His stare says 'game on', and his body language is confrontational. A wiser man would back down and refuse to acknowledge the aggressive challenge in his eyes. I've never been a wise man. All his display has earnt him is the guarantee of being in my bed tonight. My cock throbs in anticipation. No more pussyfooting around, no more backing down. If he thinks he knows the rules to this game, he's wrong.

This is my game, and it will be played by my rules.

There is no passing 'Go' to collect two hundred pounds, and no 'Get Out Of Jail Free' card. As I pick up another shot and bring it to my lips, I watch his eyes lock on the grin spreading across my face. I've just rolled double six, and he may not know it yet, but this game is already won.

# chapter 6

*Flynn*

**H**eat.
   Lips.
Tongue.
Ache.
Throb.

My dark brown eyes stare back at me from the mirror in Céline's small bathroom. Drops of water trickle down my face to land on the already damp neckline of my t-shirt and despite having escaped in here to gather my thoughts, and talk myself out of whatever is going to happen when I walk back out that door, I've yet to come up with a good excuse. My drink addled brain knows it's a bad idea. My heated skin, throbbing cock, kiss-swollen lips and frantically beating heart have other notions.

He hasn't touched me. *Yet.*

His eyes, his touch, his lips, have all been for Céline and that's the way it should be. That's the way it *has* to be. Yet, I still ache for something more.

I left them getting hot and heavy in the living room while old *Motown* classics fill the air. *Marvin Gaye* was singing *Let's Get It On* while I watched as Isaac's hands skimmed over Céline's curves and his mouth dominated hers. Taking, owning, pillaging, devouring. My dick *throbbed,* begging to be allowed in on the action and all it took was for Céline to beckon me to join them from over Isaac's shoulder and I legged it in here like a coward.

The moment we pulled up outside Celine's building in a cab, I knew I should leave. I hesitated in the front seat of the taxi as they disembarked, but instead of listening to my head, I let my feet be led by my lust and I followed them up to Céline's small apartment.

While Isaac poured drinks, Céline dimmed the lights and fiddled with the stereo until Gaye's silky smooth vocals enticed us all to begin what we came here to do.

Isaac didn't hesitate. I watched as he downed his drink without removing his eyes from the show Céline was creating. Her hips began to sway to the beat of the music, the centre of the room her stage from which to enrapture us. While his eyes were transfixed by the movements of her hands as they drifted over her skin, my eyes were locked on him. Two purposeful steps were all it took for him to reach her, wrap his arms around her waist and drag her body towards his until they were flush against each other. With his strong thigh between hers, pressing up against the soft flesh at the apex of her legs, she let out a husky moan and dropped her head back, exposing her throat for the taking. I felt every glide of his tongue along her skin as if it were me in his arms. Every time he dragged her covered pussy over the firm muscles of his thigh, I felt the friction against my cock. I was coming undone, and I hadn't yet been touched. All it took was for Céline to open her eyes and invite me to join them and I lost it. I fought through the fog of my desire and instead of walking into the seductive scene playing out in front of me, I left the room.

My traitorous body cursed every step I took away from them. My weak lungs refused to drag in enough air, and my pulsing cock throbbed so hard it hurt, but it was the organ hidden in my chest, encased in a cage of bones, sinew, veins and turbulent confusion that threatened my control more than anything else.

I was so turned on I couldn't see straight. I was so torn up inside and repulsed at myself that I wanted to walk away and never look back.

*Why?*

Why this man? Why this need? From where did this fucked up attraction stem?

I don't want him.

I don't want him.

*Liar.*

*Liar.*

*Liar.*

46

*"Fuck!"* I roughly drag my hands down my face once more and stare at the pathetic man that mocks me from the mirror.

I couldn't tell you what changed at that moment, what made me spin around and stride from the room with determined resoluteness.

Nothing? Everything? Whatever the fuck it is has me rounding the corner with one hand on the button of my jeans and the other pushing against my aching cock.

What greets me has me stopping dead in my tracks.

Isaac is naked from the waist up. His firm, sculpted chest practically glistens in the dim light. His hands are in the front pockets of his jeans stretching the fabric across his groin and highlighting his obvious need. His head is bowed, eyes closed while he listens for the change in music and just as the unmistakable opening notes of *Cry To Me* by *Solomon Burke* erupt from the speakers, his head lifts and his eyes open to land on me. The song, made famous by *that* scene with *Patrick Swayze,* a song I know well as it's one of my mother's favourites, skitters over me, piercing straight through my chest and exposing everything I've tried and failed to hide.

I *want* a man. I want *this* man.

Céline turns towards us from her position at the stereo, and I glimpse a knowing look on her face as she walks back to Isaac with a seductive smile that is solely aimed at me. She's challenging me to join them, forcing me to admit that I'm interested in more than her in this threesome.

I can barely catch a breath as I watch her step in front of

him, her movements slow, as she gently smooths her palms over his chest, fluttering her fingers across his collarbone, before curling one over his shoulder and into the hair at the nape of his neck.

His hands land on her hips, but his eyes remain on me as he once more slips his thigh between her legs and begins to move both their bodies to the music. They grind against each other as their hips move as one to the melody. Céline presses herself tightly against the bulge of his straining cock and leans back so she can look at me while rubbing herself on him.

"Join us, *Mon Cheri,*" she mouths at me, her eyes hooded with desire as she grinds herself harder on Isaac's length while he begins to rock her against him in sync with the beat. Her mouth finds his neck and his hands latch onto the hem of her sweatshirt before he drags it over her head, leaving her in just a plain white bra. Still, their bodies remain fixed together, their hips swaying, gyrating against one another in a motion that hints at the things to come.

During all of this, his eyes never leave mine. Not even for a second. He's goading me, enticing me, daring me to move and expecting me to leave. It's that thought that pushes me into action. I'm not going to do what he expects. If he thinks I'm going to run just because of this weird thing between us, he's wrong.

He grabs her leg, hooking it behind the knee and lifting it from the floor. The move allows him to lean her body further backwards so that her pussy rubs perfectly against him, eliciting a gasp of arousal to fall from Céline's lips and five slow steps forward from me. I make sure to force my internal struggle from my features and replace it with the need that burns through my veins, allowing him to see every promise of what is about to come. When I reach their melded bodies, instead of coming behind Céline and sandwiching her further into him, I keep walking. Stretching out my fingers I allow them to graze the firm curve of her hip before I feather them across her leg until they are touching his denim clad thigh. Our eye contact breaks when I continue to step around him; my hand follows my movement to purposely trail along the waist of his jeans before dropping down to touch the well-rounded globe of his arse in a sweeping caress. *Solomon Burke* sings about loneliness being a waste of time as my other hand lands on his upper back, and my greedy fingers stroke over the firm muscles covered in intricate, black scroll lettering, leaving goose bumps in their wake.

**A**cceptance is Serenity

I can't help what I do next. Seeing the raised bumps on his flesh, and the unexpected tattoo of words that both intrigue and unnerve me awakens something primal inside. A deep-seated need to taste what I'm doing to him overtakes me, and my lips quickly follow the path of my hand across his upper back and shoulders. The first contact of my mouth on his skin, just above the letter S at the start of Serenity, is my complete undoing. That and the low grumble I feel vibrating through his chest.

*You don't have to walk alone, take my hand.*

He tastes like everything I've ever wanted.

Soft, firm and smooth, with an earthy, clean undertone that makes my cock even harder, if that's possible. With a groan of my own, I slide my hands around his hips to land on Céline's, and while I pull her deeper into him, my hips push flush against his jean clad arse. My engorged cock pushes right up against his crease and like a heat seeking missile it finds its way as if it was made to settle between his firm, muscular cheeks.

All movement stops as we stand as one. Celine pressed to Isaac's front, me tight against his back, my lips a mere hairsbreadth away from the shell of his ear, my ragged breaths no doubt sending heat straight down his spine.

Then it happens.

Céline's lips find his nipple and latch on, just as his hand reaches back to grab my neck and his head twists to the side so he can pull my panting mouth to his.

If I thought I was lost before, then it was nothing compared to the way he makes me feel at this moment with his mouth claiming mine.

Heat.

Lips.

Tongue.

Ache.

Throb.

I am lost because he found me.

# chapter 7

*Isaac*

"**B**edroom."

The order is almost unintelligible as it escapes my lips on a groan.

With Céline's heat pressing against my raging cock and finally having Flynn's taste in my mouth and hard body wrapped around my back, I'm surprised I can even formulate a coherent thought.

I am seconds away from exploding in my pants like an immature teen, and moments away from saying "Fuck this" and pushing my two willing playmates to the floor. Bed be damned.

Céline's mouth leaves my nipple with an audible *pop*, and she gives me a saucy look as she trails her hands down my chest until they reach the front pockets of my jeans. Sliding a hand in each, the fingertips of her left grazes the tip of my weeping cock causing me to shudder, and her right hand grips the inner fabric to tug me forward as she takes slow, leading steps towards what I assume is her bedroom.

I go willingly. Eagerly. My feet never hesitate. I may not know exactly how this night is going to play out, but I know he's with us. He's all in. That's enough for me. I'm going to use this one night to purge Flynn Phillips from my head for good.

Cold air hits the overheated skin on my back. We've only walked forward a handful of steps, but I know Flynn hasn't followed us. Gently prising Céline's fingers from my pockets, I stop our movements and glance down at her face. All I see in her dilated pupils, swollen lips, flushed cheeks and hooded eyes is pure need and lust, no second guessing, no apprehension and no doubts. She wants this; she wants two men in her bed, but she's unaware that we've lost a player in our game for three.

"Flynn, are you coming or going?" I keep my eyes fixed on Céline as I throw the question out, not wanting to see the indecision in his features, or worse, repulsion. I've been victim to that look on his face before. He made me feel worthless. He will never get that power over me again. I'm calling the shots tonight, not him.

Céline leans around me, and I see the moment Flynn makes his decision when a wicked smile spreads her plump lips wide, her arousal heightened judging by the hitch in her breathing.

I feel his heat once more as he approaches me from behind. My body braces for his touch, my entire being frozen in anticipation.

I want his lips exploring my skin, his hands roaming every inch of me. Instead, I get a fleeting glance of his body, his stark naked and perfectly carved body, as he walks around us with his clothes balled up into one hand, and opens a door at the end of a small corridor. Hazy light spills from the opening a moment later, and Céline lets out a breathy laugh.

"I guess that's your answer."

Yes. I think the fact he's stripped and ready more than indicates Flynn's acceptance.

She once more slips her hands into my pockets, before rising up on her toes to place her mouth over mine. It's a fleeting invitation of what's to come, and I allow her to lead me in the direction of the room that a naked Flynn disappeared into only seconds ago.

She removes one of her hands as we approach the doorway, and tightens the grip of the other as she pulls me into the dimly lit room.

The bedroom is small; just enough room for a double bed, dresser and nightstand but it wouldn't make a difference how big the room was because there is one thing dominating it.

Flynn Phillips, stark bollock naked, sprawled out on his back, his deliciously tanned and sculpted body a heady contrast against the stark white cotton sheets with his hand wrapped so tightly around his eight-inch cock that it makes me see stars.

*Fuck. That. Is. Hot.*

What's even hotter is that with every drag of his tight fist over his engorged flesh his hips pump and his eyes never leave mine.

My fingers twitch to touch him.

My mouth waters to taste him.

I simultaneously lick my lips and flex my fingers, as I talk myself down from taking whatever the fuck I want from him.

Flynn's eyes flick from my eyes to my mouth and he tries and fails to stifle a moan from slipping free. The subtle groan is like a beacon for my greedy stare as I watch, utterly transfixed, as a bead of pre-cum glistens on his broad crown. The flared head of his thick cock is an angry red, visibly displaying his body's need, highlighting its desperate demand for release, urging him to blow his load no matter how hard he's trying to hold back.

My legs twitch with the need to move. I am just about to step forward and feast on what he is willingly offering me when Céline moves first.

Since the moment we stepped into the room and my eyes landed on Flynn, all thoughts of her disappeared. I forgot we were three and judging by the wicked look she throws over her shoulder at me, just before she crawls onto the bed at Flynn's feet, I'd say she's more than aware that she'd been forgotten and she is not going to allow us to disregard her again.

Flynn's eyes briefly flick towards her, but the moment she wraps her plump mouth over the swollen head of his erection, they once more latch back onto me and doesn't that make my cock very fucking happy indeed.

If he wants to think of me despite having a smoking hot woman milking him with her mouth, then I'll willingly give him a show. One he will think about for a long time to come.

I step forward until my shins press up against the edge of the bed. If I wanted to, I could reach out and caress Céline's body and maybe I will, once I ease the throbbing in my shaft that is relentlessly pounding at the zipper of my jeans, demanding to be set free.

With sure, steady fingers I pop open the top button of my jeans and drag down the zip so it opens tooth by tooth. Each millimetre the denim loosens is excruciating, but the ache in my throbbing cock is worth it to watch Flynn's desperate gaze as he tracks the movement with hungry eyes. Knowing he can't look away only heightens my need, and my cock makes its presence known as soon as the zip ends by forcing its way through the opening. Yeah, I often go commando. I've never liked the restriction of underwear, plus, at times like this, it's extremely convenient. As soon as the flushed head of my swollen cock pokes it way out of the fabric, pointing out the direction it's begging to go, Flynn's eyes flare wide with arousal. He fucking likes what he sees and damn if that doesn't make my eager shaft grow another inch under his perusal.

Céline must do something wicked to him with her

mouth because just as I'm about to push the denim off my hips, his entire lower body thrusts upwards from the bed, gagging Céline on his cock in the process.

This is obviously not her first rodeo, and she takes the violent assault on the back of her throat like a champ, gagging just once before shifting her position, relaxing her jaw, and opening her throat to suck him to the very back. The erotic onslaught of Céline's talented mouth is his undoing. I watch as he desperately tries to maintain his gaze on me, but when Céline's throat closes around his length, and she has him swallowed down from root to tip, he cannot stop his eyes from closing tightly or his head from throwing back. He growls out his release and spills every last drop into her eager mouth.

His whole body tightens as wave after wave of ecstasy rolls over him, his hips frantically shaking with the power of his orgasm, and Céline never once stops her ministrations, her desire evident as she practically purrs around his pulsing shaft.

I want to join her, want to bring him down from his rapturous high and clean him off with my lips and tongue. I want to take his softening length and languidly lick and nip and suck until he is once again hard. Hard and needy and only for me.

My knee hits the mattress just as clarity washes over Flynn.

I can see it clearly in the way his body freezes before going rigid. He squirms out from under Céline, his eyes never again finding mine and the atmosphere in the room changes from hot, heavy and laced with lust, to frigid, awkward and so cold I have to fight back a shiver, between one blink and the next.

*No, no, no, no.*

He doesn't get to do this again. He doesn't get to use any part of me to get off and then do a fucking runner with disgust in his eyes and cruel words on his lips.

"Don't you fucking dare, Flynn Phillips."

The anger in my demand radiates throughout the room. Céline stills, her head whipping towards me, confusion evident on her face but I couldn't give a fuck about her right now. My rage is aimed entirely at the man now standing with his back to me, his shoulder squared, his hands working quickly to pull on his tight black boxers. The sight of his firm glutes, moments before he covers them fully, does nothing to quell the ache in my furious cock. It still pounds with a need for this man, despite me knowing exactly what is going to happen next. The same fucking thing that happened last time. He's going to lash out and then run.

"You don't fucking get to do this again, Phillips. Are you a man or a damn mouse? Because right now all I see is a coward about to run away with his tail between his fucking legs."

That gets the reaction I want.

I see it in the rippling of his muscles before he drags his shirt over his head and spins to pin me with an icy glare.

His furious eyes bore into mine, his lips curling into a

sneer and I wait for the poison to drip from his mouth.

"Fuck you, Isaac. You don't know me, and I owe you fuck all. Now get out of my way so I can leave. I should never have come here with you. It was a mistake."

"No. You're wrong. You do fucking owe me." I grip my solid length angrily and twist my hand around its girth. His eyes flick down to the movement, and for a split second, they flare at the sight of me with my cock tightly in my fist. Any arousal in his look is instantly replaced with disgust.

"Huh." His tone is filled with contempt, derision dripping from that one syllable as his eyes pin me with a glare.

"You think I want your cock? You think I came here to fuck you or let a faggot suck me off?" The laugh that follows is vile and mocking.

"Oh, yeah. I forgot. Isaac Fox sucks cocks by pretending to be bi. You say I'm a fucking coward, yet you're too much of one to own the fact that you like dicks, not pussy."

He takes a step forward into my space, expecting me to shrink back from the bile pouring from his lips and the hate burning from his eyes.

With a prod to my bare chest he continues, "Men like you make me fucking sick. If you yearn to be another man's bitch, fucking own it. Hiding behind vagina, claiming not to be a filthy fucking homo, is pathetic." Another, more aggressive prod to my chest follows. "Poofs who pretend to be bi are full of bullshit. You are manipulative predators, you're not confused, you know exactly what you're doing."

His final angry poke to my chest is my undoing and my

hand snaps up to grip his wrist.

"Don't you fucking dare talk to me about confusion. I accept what I am and who I want. Pity you can't be so honest with yourself."

He snatches his arm from my hold as if my touch burns and steps back. With the promise of violence in his steely eyes, I further goad him by never once backing down.

"Don't fucking breathe near me ever again." His parting words before he barges past me, his shoulder checking mine in an attempt to knock me off balance.

I stand firm; my fists clench with the need to lash out, but it's my traitorous cock, still thick, still tall, still proud, still fucking throbbing, that pisses me off more.

Why the fuck would I still want someone who is filled with so much venom? Someone who is so confused by his desires that he needs to label me disgusting to assuage his personal doubts.

I am done with being judged by anyone.

Where is the community for people like me?

Gay men think I want to hide behind my attraction to women like I'm in some kind of fictional closet. Straight men believe that it's a load of bollocks and that being bi is a more acceptable version of being gay. And then we have women; well, they are intrigued mostly, but that wears off when they decide I'm an unworthy partner because not only may I stray with another woman, but I may also leave them for another man.

That's why I don't do relationships.

Bisexual is another term for confused or untrustworthy. When in truth it means I see beauty in all. I don't discriminate in my attraction. People turn me on.

Not just women.

Not just men.

Humans.

I see beauty. They see distrust.

Labels are for fucking jars, not people.

I've accepted who I am and I'll be damned if I allow a bigoted, likely closeted, prick like Flynn Phillips to belittle me again. Those moments of connection, where a spark shot straight from him into me, mean nothing. It was physical attraction, and fucked-up pheromones, nothing more nothing less.

"Well, that was unexpected, *Mon Amour.*"

Yet again, I've forgotten about Céline.

I turn to her and can't help the nervous laugh that escapes. It bubbles over the residual anger that still floods my veins when my eyes find her shocked ones.

"Yeah, you can say that again."

We both hear the front door of the apartment slam closed, and with a shrug of her shoulders and a grin on her lips she says, "Well, that was unexpected, *Mon Amour.*"

Hearing her say it again, followed by a cheeky, knowing smile pulls a genuine laugh from my chest.

"Come on, *Mon Cherie*," I tease in a bad French accent. "I need a stiff drink."

She looks purposefully down at my hard cock and then

back to my face. "You sure you wouldn't rather put something else that's stiff to good use?"

I shake my head as I pull up my jeans and gingerly tuck my hard-on away before zipping up.

"He-" I point at the offending body part, "-doesn't know when to give up, but trust me, a drink is all I need right now."

She huffs playfully, "Shame. I guess Flynn's little strop cock-blocked everyone bar him. Greedy fool."

"Yeah, a fool is right." I extend my hand for her to take and she gracefully climbs off the bed. "I'm sorry about tonight. I guess I misread the situation."

She links her arm with mine as she walks us out of the bedroom and towards the kitchen.

"Didn't we all, *Mon Cheri.* Now, you can tell me all about it, because there is most definitely a history between you both and if I'm not going to see any action myself tonight, the least I can get is some juicy details to tide me over."

She removes her hold on me and slides onto a barstool before pouring us both a generous serving of whisky.

"You owe me, Isaac. So bottoms up, then spill your guts."

I've never told anyone about that night just over a year ago and as I knock back over half of the drink before me, I decide Céline is as good as anyone to purge every detail I have on Flynn Phillips.

I hope by freeing the memory from my chest, I'll get some sort of cathartic release. I hope that saying the words out loud will be enough to sever this destructive connection we have between us.

Nothing good can ever come from wanting a man like Flynn Phillips.

The tattoo across my back itches with a phantom ache as I tell Céline about the first time I shared a bed with Flynn and another woman, about the taste of him on my tongue and about the heavy, thick and dark confusion that blanketed me for months afterwards.

When the last detail leaves my lips, when I spill the words that I allowed to affect me more than any other hurtful comments ever have, I don't feel lighter.

I feel empty.

# chapter 8

*Flynn*

It's been two months since the night I spent with Isaac and Céline. Over sixty days of self-hatred wrapped up nice and tight with a big red bow of regret and disgust.

I hate him for everything he did and didn't do.

I hate myself more.

I should have enough compunction for all of us. I should be able to make right the wrongs, contact Isaac and at least offer an apology.

But I can't.

The simple fact is that I'm a fucking coward just like he said.

My thoughts are a mutable, inconsistent and fickle presence during the day, but it's at night when I punish myself the most.

# one

I either drink myself into a stupor or pick up a willing body- a willing *female* body- to lose myself in until morning.

It doesn't help, though. Nothing helps.

I keep going through the motions. Day-by-day my "brand' soars, my business grows, and more and more people want a piece of Flynn Phillips.

If only they knew that this perfect body houses a less than perfect man. Would they buy my books, download my videos and invite me on their TV shows if they knew the fucked up man inside?

The laughable thing is, my last big feature was to be interviewed for *G.A.Y.* magazine. It seems I've become something of a gay icon. Can you say, hypocrite?

So here I am, a two-faced, bigoted charlatan, deceiving an entire community with my bright smile on the cover of their best-selling publication.

Inside the pages, my ripped body is sprayed with oil as I smile brazenly into the camera flaunting my straight guy image with a heavy dose of 'I'm comfortable in my sexuality, please lust after me.'

I fucking disgust myself.

"It's your hottest shoot yet, Flynn." Elaina teases me as she pretends to fan her face with her hand. "The pink pound is yours for the taking. Once you crack this market as a straight man, the world is your oyster."

"Yeah, I guess." I rub this morning's hangover from my

eyes with the heels of my hands, my tongue thick and dry in my arid mouth, my brain rattling against my skull to the beat of a techno playlist.

"Here, drink up."

Elaina thrusts a mug of black coffee in my face, the rich aroma testing the limits of my stomach as it churns and threatens to expel the distillery that I drained dry last night.

I lift my red-rimmed eyes to hers, and she looks down at me without an ounce of empathy, a smug smile on her lips, her face mocking the pain behind my eyeballs and the cramps in my stomach.

"Self-inflicted, no sympathy from me, you know this, Flynn. Now drink up, I've got less than an hour to get you to your first appointment of the day."

Why did I employ her as my assistant? It's never a good idea to work with family or friends and seeing as Elaina has been my best friend since childhood, you'd think I'd know she was never going to coddle me or bow down to my whims.

I groan and reach for the mug, forcing myself to sip the tar-like substance. Fuck, that's strong.

"Can't I get milk in my coffee? You know I'm more of a latte than espresso lover, yet you insist on giving me this shit. I could repair half the tarmac in London with this." I take another sip of the thick, bitter liquid and grimace as it slides down my throat.

"Well, when you grow up and stop getting wasted on a school night, I'll stop needing to sober you up the next day."

She bustles around the living room of the apartment we

share, picking up stray items including a lone pair of knickers that my visitor from last night must have left behind.

"Flynn! What the ever loving fuck?" She dangles the dirty lingerie from the end of stray chopstick.

*Huh.* We must have eaten Chinese food last night, that would explain the extra queasiness I feel today, my body isn't used to the excess carbs, fat and MSG.

"I go away for a few days, and all hell breaks loose. Can you refrain from bringing dirty bints back to our place? Just thinking of the places I may find bodily fluids is bringing me out in hives. You want to stick your todger inside rotten floozies, then book a hotel room."

She flings the pink lace underwear, and they hit me smack in the face before landing inside my half-finished mug of coffee.

"She was a primary school teacher, not a dirty bint." Using a pincer grip, I remove the now sodden knickers, and they drop onto the low table before me with a wet squelch.

"Good for her. That doesn't make her any less of a slag, leaving her filthy undies on a stranger's living room floor."

I don't bother arguing when Elaina is pissed off with me; it's a pointless exercise. Milly was sweet and loved her job in the local primary school. She was also a devil between the sheets and the scratch marks across my back prove it. She also did nothing for me, nothing at all.

Sure, I got hard, and my body found its release, but I had to close my eyes to achieve orgasm and think of shoulder-length dark hair, soulful hazel eyes, a firm rump you could bounce a penny off and a thick, silken cock beaded with arousal at the tip.

*Isaac Fox.*

He's like a fucking parasite, invading my thoughts even when I don't want him there.

"Shower, shit, shave. You've got thirty minutes, and then we're out of here whether you're ready or not."

Elaina's demand pierces through my thoughts as I sit staring blankly at the coffee stained thong.

"Yes, boss." I snark back impotently, before standing and stretching out my sore muscles.

I haven't been training as much as I should, and my body feels the loss acutely. Although my lean, well-muscled frame isn't showing neglect, I can feel it radiating from within.

I have to stop doing this shit or else it could cost me everything I've worked so hard for up to now.

I turn and walk towards my room, my bare back on full display.

"Oh, for fuck's sake. Did you have to let the dirty school teacher mark you up like *Freddy Kruger?*"

I stop and twist my head in a futile attempt to look at my back from over my shoulder. Why I bother with the gesture, I don't know because I can already feel the scratches itching as they start to scab over. Like I said, she was wild in bed.

When I shrug at Elaina, she dramatically huffs in reply and goes back to cleaning up my mess.

I amble through my darkened bedroom that stinks of sweat and sex, passing the rumpled bed and straight into my bathroom. On auto-pilot I do as instructed, and after a swift and frigid shower, I emerge damp but slightly more human.

I'm briskly drying off my hair when Elaina walks into the bathroom. She doesn't knock or announce her presence; it's just the way she is, and it's never bothered me, until now.

"Have you heard of boundaries? Privacy?"

"Have you heard of get stuffed?"

"*Jesus Christ,* Lei. Can't I have even a minute to myself?"

She stops what she's doing and peers up at me. Her elfin features soft even in the harsh florescent lighting of the bathroom.

"That's the first time you've called me Lei in months."

"No, it's not," I mumble, continuing to dry off my hair with a towel.

"Yeah, it is, Flynn. For months you've been shut off and locking me out. I haven't been your friend called Lei, I've been Elaina, your annoying assistant."

"Don't be stupid."

She steps forward and places her warm hand on the cool skin of my forearm.

"It's the truth. Where have you been Flynn? Because you haven't been present for weeks. In fact, you haven't been here with me for *months.*"

I drop the towel and look down at her hand. The warmth of her touch penetrates right down into my bones. Is it true? Have I been detached? Absent from the only true friendship I have?

Everyone wants a piece of me. I'm prime real estate. I'm

Flynn Phillips, the hot new thing with the firm body and bulging bank account.

But not Lei.

She's seen me with nothing.

She was my everything when my life fell apart. She was the only one there for me when I lost not only my hero but a part of my parents too. When I wanted nothing more than to check out of life, she brought me back to the living.

She held me, comforted me, loved me, when the crippling whys threatened to rip me to shreds from the inside out because all of a sudden he was gone. Gone and no one knew why.

I miss him. I miss him so fucking much that even thinking of him makes it harder to breathe.

Even now my life is divided.

There's before.

Then there's after.

The two are entwined yet so far apart that they cannot exist side by side.

I fight the memories because I cannot take the pain. It's a constant battle between remembering and forgetting. Between before and after.

Elaina's small hand stills mine. I've been absentmindedly twisting the leather bracelet around my wrist, feeling the worn, knotted plait beneath my fingers, fighting back seventeen years of memories.

"It's okay to think about him, to miss him."

I jerk my arm back, and her hand drops loosely to her

side.

Her wide, pleading eyes stare up at me, a watery sheen turning the dark green orbs murky but nonetheless beautiful.

"He wouldn't want this for you, Flynn. It's been ten years, and you still won't say his name. Say it with me now. Cl…"

"*Stop.* Don't… I…"

"He didn't intend to wound you, Flynn. His hurt was just too much, he…"

"Don't you dare tell me how to feel. He left us. His selfishness left behind a pain worse than just the initial shock and devastation. It left behind a never ending ache that will never go away. It will never fade because we will never know."

I spin around to look in the mirror and stare at a face so similar, yet so different to his.

"We will never know why, and the agony we will always carry is because of everything that will never be. It is more than pain, it's crippling."

She places her palms flat against my back and rests her forehead against my clammy skin.

"Then just imagine his pain. It was too much for him to bear. Nobody willingly abandons the ones they love Flynn."

She places one soft kiss between my shoulder blades and leaves me.

Leaves me with possibly the two most meaningless and nondescript words in the English language, 'what' and 'if'. The trouble stems from putting them both together. Side by side they have the power to haunt every aspect of your life.

What and if.

What if?

What.

If.

"What's on the schedule today?"

After my pathetic mini-breakdown that I'm going to attribute to a raging hangover, I push any and all painful thoughts aside and bury the memories threatening to flood my carefully constructed world.

We're in the back of a taxi, heading God knows where, but I know Elaina has everything under control and isn't holding this morning against me.

She pulls out her tablet and after a few swipes reads out today's agenda.

"We're headed to *Women's Daily*, for your weekly cooking and nutrition slot, then straight from the studio to an interview with a men's health magazine followed by a four o'clock meeting with the *Wicked Water* reps for a final image approval."

"What?" I snap my head away from the dreary view outside my window where I was aimlessly watching the world go by and stare at Elaina.

"I said…"

"I heard what you said. I didn't know we had a *Wicked Water* meeting. I thought all that was wrapped up?"

She looks over at me with an expression that says 'I give up on you sometimes' and replies, "We always get the final say on images, Flynn. It's standard protocol. But because you're the star of this campaign they want to schmooze you and keep you happy."

"Cancel it."

It's her turn to snap her head towards mine.

"I can't."

"Yes, you can. I don't want to waste my time in that meeting."

Her pretty eyes harden, and she fires back "Oh, no? Would you rather use your precious time to trawl for skanks or drink yourself into oblivion? I'm not cancelling. Grow the fuck up."

Anger, frustration and a hefty dollop of anxiety war for dominance in my gut.

I want to ask if he will be there but I can't risk revealing anything, not even to Lei.

*Fuck. My. Life.*

I pray for divine intervention. Anything to get me out of that meeting at four o'clock. I cannot be in the same room as Isaac Fox ever again.

# chapter 9

## *Isaac*

"Did your father show you the snaps from the cruise?"

I glance up from my tablet where I'm checking my schedule for today and watch my mother as she prepares breakfast for her 'two remaining men', as she calls us. She means my father and me, seeing as all my brothers have flown the nest.

"Yes. Twice. They were riveting," I reply with humour thickening my voice.

"Oh hush, they aren't that bad. Okay, he took a lot of sunsets and boats, but we both know where you got your artistic flair from and it wasn't your father." She winks at me over the steaming pan of scrambled eggs before turning to squeeze some fresh juice.

"I'm heading over to Josh and Laura's later. Josh

mentioned you have something for him." She places a steaming plate of food before me and a small glass of fresh orange. Being the last son at home certainly has its benefits.

"Yeah, I'll grab it from my room. It's just an IOU certificate for studio time when the new baby arrives. I thought it would make a great pre-baby gift, plus I feel a little guilty that I missed the whole baby shower get together when I was called away the other month."

"That's a fabulous idea, darling. I know they loved the shots you took of Ivy when she was a newborn."

"Yeah, well. It's the least I can do. Besides, isn't Laura well past her popping date?"

My mother raises her eyebrows as she sits opposite me and begins to sip her tea. "Women don't pop, Isaac. It's much more painful than that. I sometimes wonder how I ended up with five of you. Every time I gave birth I told your father that was the last. And, yes, Laura is four days overdue. Josh said she's getting anxious which is why I'm going to sit with her today for a few hours while he's in work. Isn't it ridiculous that fathers are only allowed time off *after* the baby makes an appearance? What about supporting their families? It seems a double standard to me."

I'm barely paying attention to her words because my eyes have just landed on the appointment that's plotted into my diary for four o'clock today.

**4 PM Wicked Water – Head Office, Davenport Square**

"What's wrong, darling? You look like someone just stole your camera and dropped it over the side of *London Bridge*."

Her words are meant to make me smile, but the churning in my gut makes that an impossibility.

"Isaac?"

I lift my head and look over at my mother. Her face is a perfect representation of each one of us. When I look at her, I see home, family, security and love.

"Just work stuff, nothing important. I'll go and grab that certificate before I head out. My day is jam packed, so I'd best get a head start."

I push my stool back from the breakfast bar and grab a piece of toast to go.

"All work and no play…"

"Yeah, yeah. I know. I'm okay, Mum. I promise."

She looks me over thoughtfully, her eyes lingering on my face, studying my features.

"It's more than that. I see you thrive under pressure when it's just work related stress. Whatever this is it's leaving dark circles under your eyes and a heavy burden on your shoulders."

Damn, my mother has always been too perceptive for her own good.

"Ma, it's…"

"Please don't insult me by telling me it's fine, or that you're fine or any other version of the word fine. I'm a woman, we invented the use of the word fine, when, in fact, everything is far from being fine."

I laugh lightly and shake my head. "I was going to say it's all good. Nothing to worry about. You're the one with an issue with the word fine."

She narrows her eyes at me in consternation. "And you're deflecting, very poorly, I might add."

I turn my eyes away from her face and drag my hand through my hair. It tangles at the ends, and I have to tug with some force to remove my fingers from the knots.

"I need a haircut."

"*Isaac.*" She uses that tone, the one you've heard your entire childhood and even as an adult it makes you stop in your tracks.

I turn my head to face her once more. Her eyes now searching mine, attempting to pry out all the things I hold back.

"I can't stop thinking about someone. Someone who is no good for me and when I say no good, I mean on every level. He's…"

My sentence drops off as I try and search for the words to finish.

"The one."

"No." the word erupts from my lips like a curse.

"We're like fire and gasoline. He will burn me alive, and I will only fuel the flames."

She's quiet for a moment, absorbing my words.

I wait, hoping for some wisdom, hoping for someone to tell me what to do.

"Then walk away, before you both end up reduced to

ash."

"I have. There's nothing between us."

She slowly rises from her seat and walks towards me, her palm reaches up and cradles my cheek.

"Oh, my sweet boy. When there's as much heat between you as you've just admitted, I wouldn't call that nothing."

Her lips turn up slightly on the corners as I lean in to her comfort and she continues, "The sun is in the sky for a reason. It brings life, it brings warmth, and without it, we wouldn't be here. But just like the sun, something's cannot be looked at directly as they can make you go blind. Is he no good for you or are you allowing yourself to be blinded by something else?"

An hour later, I'm leaving my parents' house on the back of my motorbike. It isn't often I get to take out my *Kawasaki Zephyr* because I normally have my camera and equipment with me, but today is full of meetings, including the last one of the day when I may come face to face with Flynn Phillips.

Maybe that's the main reason I take the bike instead of calling for a cab, this way I can make a speedy getaway if needed.

I lift my hand and flip down my visor, waving to my mother as she pulls away in her car to go and spend the day with Laura.

I bet Josh is on pins waiting for the new arrival. He's

never liked feeling impotent and unable to control things, but he's just going to have to let nature take its course this time. Poor bloke.

At least my problems are somewhat under my control.

Even if Flynn attends in person today, it doesn't mean I can't keep my distance and remain professional. The fact that I haven't been with anyone else since that night is irrelevant, I've just been busy and in a different country almost every other day.

*Like that's ever stopped you before.*

*L*unchtime comes and goes. The morning is spent showing my portfolio and mock-ups for a new ad campaign for a high street clothing store. I leave the meeting feeling buoyed. They loved my ideas, and I get to work with some amazing people that I have admired from afar but never had the chance to work with before.

Lunch is a quick sandwich and coffee to go, which I consume on the back of my bike before I head off to meet Jake's wife Emma at his new production company. JF Global is a new addition to his steadily growing brand. Not only is my brother the hottest actor on the planet right now, but he's also a business-savvy entrepreneur with his fingers is so many pies I'm surprised he can keep track. He hires me for everything. There's nothing better than a healthy dose of nepotism. If the Fox family can keep things in-house, we strive to do so, it's the perks of being one part of a successful family, I guess.

Jake won't be in attendance today because he's currently filming some major feature film in the wilds of Brazil, but I know Emma is more than capable of running their business without him. In fact, it's her smiling face that greets me as I pull up right outside the front doors of the building just fifteen minutes later.

"Hey, Iz. It's been too long. I haven't seen you since the wedding." She brings me in tight for a hug before releasing me.

"Thanks for the beautiful wedding album and the canvas. I never realised you even took that shot."

She's thanking me for the pictures of their wedding, and the unguarded, intimate shot of them that I took just moments before they left the reception.

Emma is sat sideways across Jake's lap, her dress trailing across the floor in delicate waves. Her arm is around his neck, while his hands hold her waist and they lean into each other forehead to forehead their eyes seeing no one but each other, it's as if there is no one else in the room. No, it's more than that, it's as if they are the only two people left on the planet. The look of love on their faces radiates outwards eclipsing everything else.

I had the image made into a large canvas, and from what my mother has said, it sits proudly on the wall of their living room.

"Thanks for letting me be a part of your day. Honestly, it was my pleasure." It's the truth. That day changed me somehow.

"So," I step out of her embrace and link my arm through hers. "There's still time to ditch my big brother and fall helplessly in love with his younger, more charismatic sibling."

She knows I'm teasing and plays along, guiding me through the reception area into the offices beyond.

"Do you mean Liam? Because I think he's got himself tangled up with another woman."

"Try again," I interject with a huff.

"Well, you can't be talking about Josh, everyone knows he only has eyes for Laura." Even without looking at her face I know she's smiling.

"You wound me." I raise my hand and place it across my heart dramatically.

"And that is why you're not the actor in the family. I've seen more realistic performances in *Sharknado*."

"Shut up. It wasn't that bad." I'm semi-serious. I thought I nailed that pretty bloody well.

She chuckles before walking through the door of her office and sitting down on the sofas that take up a large corner of the room.

"It wasn't that good, either. Let's just say that Jake takes pictures about as well as you act."

Jake cuts the heads off people and blurs most frames.

"Yeah, okay. I'll give you that. So, what have you got for me today?"

She picks a small file from the table and hands it over.

"We need location shots for the indie-film Jake is

desperate to make. He wants to direct it and is looking for some complete unknowns to take the leads. He wants to give someone a break. It's his pay it forward I guess."

I read over the brief synopsis of the film; it sounds bloody amazing. Three men in a dark and dangerous world, trying to take down a secret organisation from the inside out. Fighting against their own flesh and blood to restore order and protect the innocent. It's dark, and it's gory, and it sounds fucking epic.

There's a lead role for a *Cole Hunter* and another for a *Faye Craven*. Even the secondary roles for his brother and trusted friend sound gritty, twisted and all kinds of messed up. Messed up in a seriously good way.

"This looks amazing. Has Jake found his leads yet?"

She smiles proudly before replying, "Not yet, once his current shoot wraps up it's his next project. He's really excited about this. I am too."

Emma's face is filled with adoration and love just speaking about her husband. It fills me with a yearning. I want someone to look just like that when they talk about me. And isn't that just a scary fucking thought.

Uncomfortable with the way my mind is heading, I stand, close the file and tuck it under my arm.

"I'll get right on those locations. I may also have a few others that could work, so I'll scout those out next week and have them ready for when Jake returns."

"Thanks, Iz. He hoped you'd be excited about this. He's planning on asking you to take on the cinematographer's role, so if it's something you'd want to try your hand at, the job is yours. Jake was going to ask you himself when he gets home, but he knows how busy you are right now and wanted me to plant the seed before you're booked up for the next five years solid."

*Wow.* That would be amazing. I said I appreciated nepotism but giving me such a huge role, one I've never undertaken before, really blows me away.

"I'd…" I'm lost for words.

"You don't have to make a decision yet, just think about it." Emma offers me a kind smile and walks me towards the door.

Finally finding my tongue I answer, "No, tell Jake I want it."

She stops before reaching for the handle and turns to look at me.

"Why don't you tell him yourself when he comes home in three weeks. I think you should be the one to make his day. He wants this to be a family venture. I know he has plans for all of you, even Josh. Although, I'm not sure how much he will want to get involved considering the new baby and his teaching job."

Getting to work with all my brothers on one project would be the highlight of my career so far. I can see why Jake is excited about this.

"Wow. You've really changed him, you know that."

She looks thoughtfully at me before responding, "He's given me more than I ever thought I wanted. I think when you've found the person you're supposed to be with, the change comes naturally for both of you."

I'm not sure what she sees on my face, but as I move to step out of her office, her hand lands on my shoulder and she speaks softly and with meaning.

"You have to trust yourself, Iz. Nobody but you can say if something is right or wrong or if someone is right or wrong. On paper, Jake and I would look so wrong, but in life, there is nothing and no one else that could be so right, for either of us."

I leave the JF Global offices excited for the new project, confused about Emma's words and yet hopeful.

That is until my phone chimes with an alarm to remind me of my next meeting.

*Flynn Phillips.*

He's so very wrong for me in every way, on and off paper. I just hope he's not at the *Wicked Water* meeting. If I can avoid him, surely, one day soon I'll remove the ache of him from my chest, the touch of his lips will erase itself from my skin and the image of him in my bed will dissolve from my mind.

*Nothing and no one else could be so right.*

Emma's words rattle around, over and over again in a continuous loop. She's wrong, everyone can see that her and Jake are meant to be, whereas, put me in a room with Flynn Phillips and brace yourself for carnage.

# chapter 10

*Flynn*

Tap. Tap. Tap.

My leg will not keep fucking still, and as it relentlessly bounces under the table, my fingers keep the same rhythm on the wooden surface above.

Elaina glares at me across the table, her eyes warning me to get it together. I can only imagine what I must look like, nervous, sweaty, fidgeting like a junkie in detox itching for my next fix.

"Another drink anyone?" Karl, one of the *Wicked Water* reps asks.

Elaina politely declines while I just shake my head, my whole body vibrating with the need to get the fuck out of here. I glance at the clock directly above Karl's head. He's late. Twenty-five minutes late.

Joel, another company rep, re-enters the room and closes the door behind him before speaking.

"Unfortunately, it looks like Isaac has been delayed or is unable to attend. So shall we get this meeting started? I know we're eager to show you how fantastic this campaign is going to be."

"What? Where is he?"

The question falls out of my mouth without thought. I can't sit here like a fucking inmate on death row, just waiting for the axe to fall and for Isaac Fox to stroll into the room when I least expect it.

Joel glances awkwardly towards Karl before replying.

"We've been unable to get in touch with Isaac. He confirmed his attendance this morning but I've called him several times over the last ten minutes, and it appears his phone is switched off or unavailable. I've left a message at his studio, but I don't want to keep you waiting any longer so we'll carry on without him."

The next hour is spent listening to Karl and Joel wax lyrical about this whole ad campaign. Phrases like 'hottest promo ever' and 'sure to make everyone wet' get thrown around while they negotiate with Elaina regarding some personal appearance for when the adverts and billboards go live across the U.K. in a couple of weeks' time. I sit in silence, smiling when I think I should, nodding when asked if I like something, generally ignoring everything going on around me.

My head is stuck, fixated on the man who isn't even in

the room. Seriously, I am beyond fucked up.

The only thing I genuinely take an interest in are the images. I knew Isaac was at the top of his game, but these photographs eclipse anything else I've ever done before. They are too good to advertise some posh water brand, they deserve to be given acclaim and adorn gallery walls for the whole world to see his talent.

"Can I take these with me?" The room falls silent at the first sentence to come out of my mouth for almost the entire meeting. Lifting two of my favourite images, I hold them up in question.

"Sure, sure," Karl flusters, followed by a "Take as many as you want," from Joel.

So I do just that. I gather up every image laid out before me and stand, indicating that I'm done here.

"If we've covered everything, I'll leave you with Elaina to finish off."

She gapes at me, about to open her mouth and curse me out but her professionalism wins over, and she nods tightly, her eyes boring into mine, threatening all kinds of retribution when she gets me alone.

I briskly shake both men's hands as I leave the room with my haul of photographs tucked safely under my arm. It's only when I exit the building, and my feet hit the pavement outside, that I take my first full breath.

This needs to stop.

This situation is all my fault. Not Isaac's, not Céline's, and certainly not Elaina's.

I am the one with the ability to end this.

This is not who I am. I hate the person I've become over the last few weeks. I've always been the fun-loving, hard-working, fitness enthusiast who worked hard and played hard.

The self-destructive arsehole currently inhabiting my body needs to be extinguished.

No more.

Time to draw a line under it. I'm done.

"**Y**ou fucked up today."

"I know."

"It's time to get your shit together Flynn and either tell me what's going on or get over it."

"I know that too."

I raise myself over the bar for one last chin lift and drop down to the floor, grabbing my towel before turning to face my best friend.

She looks up at me with a mixture of worry and hurt flashing in her eyes. I know I hurt her when I lock her out, but she knows that's my way. I'm not a spill my guts kind of person.

"It was a blip. I'm over it. Normal service shall be resumed."

I give her a cheeky smile hoping to break the tension, but she just looks sadly at me.

"You know what? One day soon, every poisonous thing

that you keep bottled up inside is going to spill out. The longer you let it fester and grow, the uglier that moment will be."

She turns to leave the room that I converted into my personal gym. It's the biggest room in the whole apartment, and it's the place where I retreat when I need to not only work out my body but also my mind.

"I love you, Lei," I whisper to her, causing her to still in the doorway.

"I love you too, Flynn." She doesn't turn around, and part of me is relieved, the other part of me injured. I cannot afford for her to give up on me. I'll have no one left.

With sweat rolling over my skin, my breath hammering out of my lungs and my legs being tested to their limits as I pound out mile fifteen on my running machine, I vow to do better, to be better and to right all my wrongs. Starting with Elaina.

I may be unable to allow her to see inside of me, but I can still show her the man I want to be and the friend I should've always been.

Then I'll apologise to my parents for being absent from their lives these last ten years. I may have provided for them financially by paying off their debts, buying them the first home they've ever owned and making sure they will never struggle again, but I haven't been a son. In fact, that night, ten long years ago, they didn't lose just one child, they lost both of us. When he left us, shattering our family into sharp shards of pain, he took a huge part of me with him.

I can never forgive him for abandoning me, for willingly deciding that life wasn't worthy, that *we* weren't enough, and for leaving me with questions that will never be answered and an emptiness that I'll never again fill.

He gave up.

He checked out.

He said he couldn't do this anymore, and by *this* he meant life.

He couldn't do life anymore.

So we were left to try and live a life without him. A half-life of what ifs, whys, and painful memories. How can the party go on when the most vibrant, effervescent person has taken their leave? The music has died, the colours have faded, and everything is over too soon.

He said that living a lie was killing him.

He said that pretending was killing him.

He said that life was killing him.

He was tired of it all. Tired of hurting everyone he loved with his lies.

His truth hurt us more.

His truth destroyed us all.

Because it took him away.

All that was left was the thick bough of a tree, empty bottles strewn in long grass, scattered pills fallen from up high, tight rope knotted to choke and scrawled words of love that would never be enough.

# chapter 11

## *Isaac*

The call came as I was pulling to a stop in the car park of the *Wicked Water* offices.

My helmet is fitted with Bluetooth, but seeing as I was already at my destination, I pulled it off my head, attached it to my bike and strode towards the front of the building with my phone to my ear and my hand attempting to tame my wayward hair.

"Hey, Mum. I'm just heading into a meeting. Can I call you back in an hour?"

The initial silence should have given me pause. With my mind on other things specifically the man who was likely to be in the building before me, I didn't read the signs.

"Mum? Did you hear me? Listen, I think we have a bad connection. I'll call you later."

"We need you, Isaac. Josh needs you."

Her tone stops me in my tracks just meters from the front door.

"Mum?" I ask cautiously, nerves building in the back of my throat almost choking me, "What's going on?"

I don't want to ask because I know something is wrong, very very wrong and for a brief moment when faced with something bad, you want to pretend nothing's happened and that everything is okay.

But nothing is okay.

"Mum? Has Josh been hurt? Is Ivy okay? Has the baby arrived?"

Silence.

"Mum, I'm freaking out here. Talk to me."

I'm already walking away from the building back to my bike. My stomach churns before bottoming out, and despite the surrounding streets bustling with life all around me, all I feel and all I hear is silence.

A harrowing sob, the kind that comes from the depths of your belly, echoes over the phone line, followed by the choked words, "Please, Isaac." Muffled sounds crackle over the airway, the phone is taken away from my mother and handed to someone else.

"Iz, it's Emma. I'm here with Josh and your parents, so they are not alone but if you could…"

"Where are you, Emma? What the hell has happened?"

She takes a heavy breath that ripples over my skin setting my nerves on edge.

"We're at the General Hospital, Accident and Emergency. Please, if you can come quickly, I don't… I just…"

"I'm on my way, Emma. I'll be there in less than fifteen minutes."

Ten minutes later I burst through the A&E doors having broken every traffic law in the *Highway Code.*

I wait in line, stifling the urge to scream and shout at the receptionist who is tucked safely away behind her Plexiglas enclosure.

When I finally get to step up to the counter a few minutes later, I don't even know why I'm here. Nobody told me who was injured or unwell. It could be Josh, or God forbid, little Ivy.

"I… umm… had a call from my mother, I'm looking for-"

"*Isaac!*" Emma's voice cuts through the noise of the crowded waiting room, and I spin to face Jake's wife. She rushes up to me, crushing me to her in a hug so tight I can barely breathe. When she pulls away, her arms are shaking, and her face is ashen.

"What's happened, Em? Where is everyone?"

"Sir, if you're done here, step away from the counter."

The harsh voice of the hospital receptionist interjects, dragging my eyes away from Emma.

"Sorry… I… umm, I'll just get out of the way." I lead Emma away from the counter and against the nearest wall attempting to find some privacy. When I look down at her distraught face, I have that thought again, the one where you wish you could say 'don't tell me, I don't think I can bear to hear the words.'

Instead, I wrap my arms around her and pull her to my chest saying, "What's happened?"

With a deep, shuddering breath, she pulls away and looks at me with aquamarine eyes that are overflowing with unshed tears.

"It's Laura. Josh arrived home and found her asleep in bed. Your mother had only left her a few hours before as Laura said she was feeling tired and wanted to take a nap. When Josh came home he couldn't rouse her and called for an ambulance. We don't know anything yet. Josh and your parents are in the family waiting room, Liam and Nate are on their way."

"But she's okay, and the baby is okay?"

The tears that pooled in her eyes moments earlier now spill free and her face crumples.

"We don't know, they have taken her to surgery and are about to perform an emergency caesarean, but they lost her on the way here in the ambulance. They couldn't find her pulse or a heartbeat for the baby."

I know words are coming out of her mouth, but I just don't understand them. I don't understand anything.

"I don't understand."

She sobs loudly, and I realise that I need to hold this together, that I need to man up and keep my crumbling emotions in check.

"Take me to them."

I wrap my arms around her shoulder and allow her to guide me through the throngs of people, out through a set of double doors and down a long corridor. A few turns later and we arrive at a room with a sign that says 'Family Waiting Area'.

She stops outside with her hand on the door and hesitates.

"It's okay Emma. They are all going to be okay."

B roken.

Have you ever watched someone you love completely shatter before your eyes?

Have you ever felt the sharp stab of impotence because you cannot do anything, say anything or be anything that they need to get through an event that has wiped out their reason for living?

Watching my brother splinter apart in front of my eyes was a living hell for which I have no name.

It took everything I have inside me to tell myself that just being there, not healing, not curing, not making anything better, was enough.

It wasn't.

And it wasn't just Josh who was ruined.

My mother was inconsolable; my father struggling under the weight of her grief, then there was Emma, currently being comforted by Liam, my youngest brother. They have always had a close connection, siblings not by blood but by marriage.

That left Nate and me to silently stand guard over Josh.

We both sit on either side of him where he's slumped on the floor against the farthest wall. That's the place where he collapsed when the Doctors came to deliver the news we never expected. That's where he crumpled when his entire world crashed down around him and buried him alive under the rubble of shock, pain and loss. We sit immobile in the same spot, never moving, no matter what happens around us. Our hands on his body, in a futile attempt to offer comfort.

*You may not feel this way now, or for the foreseeable future, but you are not alone.*

The thing is, though, he is alone.

His grief is his alone.

His loss unlike ours.

It's catastrophic, it's all consuming, it's fucking unfair, and I want to scream at the top of my lungs at the injustice of life and the villainy of death.

What feels like hours but is likely just a few minutes later, Josh propels himself up from the floor throwing off our hands as if our touch physically burns.

"I want to see her. I *need* to see her."

His wild eyes dart around the room never landing on anyone for more than a second.

When nobody moves or answers him, his hands ball at his sides and he lets out an unearthly roar. It's as if someone else, some crazed and rage fuelled monster, has inhabited my calm, quiet brother's body.

The thing is, it has. Denial and anger have taken control of my normally placid brother and hold him in their remorseless grip.

"Take me to my *wife!*" His demand is pulled from his chest and expelled into the room with the force of a fist to everyone's guts.

"I said, *take me to my fucking wife!*"

Rage twists his handsome face into painful ugliness, and we all stare in shock and helplessness unable to find any words of comfort or aid.

Chest heaving, arms shaking, he stands before us in naked fury. The veins in his neck and forehead stand out in stark relief against his pallid skin.

As quickly as the rage takes him, it leaves.

His body, unable to contain his sorrow, slumps. His head drops to his chest and a voice saturated in pure grief utters his last plea.

"Take me to my wife. She needs me, and she's alone. She hates being alone."

I feel my own heart throb and threaten to shear itself straight through the centre. I can give him this. I can give him his one true love if only fleetingly.

Ignoring everyone else in the room because I need to keep calm and not allow the pain I will see on their faces stall me, I slowly walk up to Josh and lightly place my hand on his shoulder.

He shudders at my touch but doesn't shrug me off.

"Come with me, Josh. I'll take you to Laura. Just hold on to me, okay."

He doesn't respond or acknowledge me, but he allows me to lead him slowly from the room.

The nurse stationed at a desk a little way down the hall notices us before we get to her. She stands, sympathy flooding her features and nods in agreement before I even ask my question.

"Mr Fox?" she addresses Josh, and he lifts his head, his haunted eyes blinking just once. "Let me take you to your wife."

He nods. One pitiful movement of his head and we silently follow the nurse to a room set off from the corridor.

When she stops outside, she addresses Josh once more.

"We've made her comfortable and removed all the tubes and equipment, so she just looks like she's sleeping." Her eyes find mine before falling back to Josh. "Take as long as you need. When you're ready, I can come and get you to see your new son."

"*No.* Just leave, I just want to be alone with my wife. Both of you leave."

I open my mouth to tell him he needs to see his new baby but a quick look at the kind nurse and the slight shake of her head has me closing my mouth in silence.

"That's okay, Mr Fox. We'll leave you for as long as you

need."

She quietly pushes open the door to the dimly lit room and opens it wide for Josh to walk in.

I do not follow. He needs this time for himself. He needs to say goodbye without an audience. He needs to speak of his love freely and feel the touch of her skin one last time.

This is his last moment with the girl he has loved since the day he met her when they were both just fourteen years old.

Young love with long lives ahead of them. Plans to make, family to build, and dreams to chase.

This morning he woke up and kissed her warm lips goodbye, spoke of the future they were building and of the new life they were eager to welcome.

This evening those warm lips are now cold, and he will speak of a future in which she will not physically be present and of a child that will never know the warmth of her touch.

While he spends his last moments with the girl who stole his heart as a teenager, I will take his place and sit with his new born son.

I will watch over him, so he is not alone, and until his father returns I will tell him how much he's wanted and loved.

*L*ife gives and life takes away.

It's brutal, and it's fucking unfair, and I don't understand it, but what I do know is that it goes on with or without you.

The nurse grants my request and takes me to see my new nephew.

I sit next to his cot and look down at his mop of dark hair that is so much like Josh's and begin telling him a love story.

A story of a shy young boy and a sweet young girl and of how nothing, not even death, could kill their love.

Their love lies before me with ten tiny fingers, ten tiny toes, and a cute button nose. Their love will grow with him, and as I rest my finger next to his tiny hand, which he then grips tightly between his soft fingers, I promise him that everything is going to be okay. That his Daddy and Mummy love him.

That we love him.

Love; it's precious, it's life. Never take it for granted.

*Almost twelve months later.*

# chapter 12

*Flynn*

"That's the last of my things in the removal van. You sure you don't want me to hang around and help you finish loading yours?"

Elaina stands in our now empty living room with her hands on her hips surveying the space. It's completely barren, except for my last few boxes propped against the wall.

"Nah, I'm good. You can head off. I'm sure Jace is eager to get you all to himself."

"He's getting me all to himself for the rest of his life." She wiggles her ring finger at me; the one adorned with a rock the size of Gibraltar. "I think he can spare me for a little while longer."

I drop the last of my books into the box at my feet, dust my hands off on my jeans and walk towards where she stands.

"He's a lucky man, Lei. Now, go and begin the rest of your life and stop worrying about me." I wrap my arms around her petite frame and drag her to me for a hug.

"Besides, I'll see you again on Monday. The first day of shooting, remember? I'll need my trusty assistant slash sidekick there to hold my hand. I can't believe someone booked me for a part in a major feature film."

"Believe it, hot stuff. I told you the sky is the limit." She digs her small fingers between my ribs in a tickling motion until I shake her off. The girl is a ruthless tickler.

"Yeah, well. We'll see. At least with the amount of makeup I'll need for the role if I crash and burn I can try and deny it was me."

She stands on tiptoes and reaches up to pinch my cheeks. "I can't believe they are willingly going to disfigure all this handsomeness. I mean, who would want to scar up this pretty boy face?"

"Calling me a pretty boy is not at all demeaning. Here I thought you loved me for my wit and charm."

She laughs and pops a wet smacker on my cheek, before rubbing it off with her hand. "Yeah, well. You have that going for you too, I guess." Her face falls a little, and she adds, "Well if you're sure I can go…"

"I'm sure. Go and christen your new place with your hunky fiancé."

"I'll tell him you said that."

"What? That he's to bone you in every room?"

"No, that he's hunky."

"You do that. It's not like I could steal him away from you, that boy is smitten."

*Are you finding this conversation a little weird? Wondering how I'm so openly cool, calm and collected about my sexuality? It's not because I've admitted to Elaina about being attracted to a man, it's just that I've finally admitted it to myself and moved on. I refer to it- only in my head of course- as the Isaac Fox Effect. I've yet to have the same visceral reaction to another man. Therefore it was a freak one-off and seeing as I haven't encountered him since that night a year ago, everything is right in the world.*

*Well, all of that and the fact that I've been quietly seeing a therapist. Not just about my sexuality, about everything, including losing my brother. It helps. It helps a lot.*

"Go on now, shoo. I've got this under control. I'll see you on Monday. You can check out my new place and give it the Lei seal of approval."

"Can't wait." She blows me a kiss and calls over her shoulder, "Don't forget to drop the keys off to the concierge when you leave. You'll only complain if they charge you for changing the locks and you're in deepest darkest Wales."

"It's Cardiff. It's a bloody city."

"It's Wales. Why are they filming a movie that's set in London in bloody Wales?"

She doesn't want an answer. She's already walking out the door still mumbling something about outdoor toilets and a lack of indoor electricity. The location was her only complaint about me taking this role, despite the fact I've never acted in my life. She's fine with me playing a cold-blooded, disfigured killer, she's fine with me keeping tokens of my victims and wearing them around my neck, she's just not happy about having to commute to Wales.

I don't have the same problem. I love Wales.

As soon as Jace proposed and Elaina broke the news that they were going to live together, I rented a place out in Cardiff on a short-term lease. It makes sense, seeing as I'm going to be filming there for the next six months at least. Plus, I love the city. Having attended Cardiff Met for my Sports Science degree, I'm eager to go back as I have so many fond memories of my time there.

Warm summer days with friends on the green outside the Castle, the bustling vibrancy of Cardiff nightlife, the varied mix of Welsh heritage and culture combined with influences from all over the world. The way the city would come alive with good-humoured sportsmanship on rugby international days. I could go as far to say that, despite living in London for the last six years or so, Cardiff is my favourite city in the world. There's no place quite like it, and I can't wait to go back.

I take one last look through the apartment I've shared with Elaina for the last couple of years and smile at the memories these walls hold.

Yes, I'll be sad to let this place go, but I'm excited to start the next chapter of my life, just as Elaina is starting the next chapter of hers.

She's found the one that she's meant to travel the road

with, while I remain alone, and although I can feel my internal clock ticking telling me to settle down, I just haven't found anyone to do that with yet, and I'm okay with that. If it happens, it happens. If not, well... I have my career, and hopefully this film will be a new direction for me, as there is only so long that I can rely on my body to be my brand. I need a long-term path, and if I nail this role exciting things will follow.

I shut the door on my past and carry my last few boxes down to the van I've hired to drive all my stuff to Cardiff.

I could've had a company do all this for me, but I'm excited to take this step myself. A fresh start that will only build on all my hard work so far.

Goodbye London, Hello Cardiff.

Goodbye Flynn Phillips, fitness personality. Hello Flynn Phillips, award winning actor.

Well, you've gotta have dreams.

Aim high, dream high. Even if you're shooting for the moon but miss, you'll still end up somewhere among the stars, or so my mother was fond of telling us growing up.

Like most mothers, she's right.


Six hours later, after getting stuck in tailbacks on the dreaded M4 motorway, I pull up in front of an imposing, traditional period style house on a quiet suburban street just outside the city centre.

I could've rented a swanky apartment right in the city,

but I love this part of Cardiff. It has parks, bars and a vibrant café culture. I wanted to be within walking distance of the city but also feel like I'm removed from the hustle and bustle for a few months at least. Plus, we'll be filming on location a lot, so this will be the perfect place to escape to after a long day on set.

The estate agent is waiting for me on the doorstep. I'm sure it was my name alone that has him out here at ten o'clock at night when he should be home with his wife and kids. The hefty commission combined with a household name as a tenant is sure to look good on his portfolio of properties.

I'm not complaining, I appreciate the welcome, including a fully stocked fridge and bar of which he informs me as we enter the property.

He also let slip that a few of the other actors and the director, Jake Fox, are all staying in houses on this very same street. It's something I already knew as Jake's assistant informed me before I signed the lease, but it's a little loose-lipped of this agent to be sharing the same information, so I tell him just that, and he looks rightly apologetic.

"Yes, sorry, Mr Phillips. I guess I got carried away, but I'm sure that seeing as you're working with Mr Fox, he won't mind me letting you know that you are neighbours."

I glare in response, turning my back on his attempt at schmoozing his way out of it and instead surveying the inside of my new home.

High ceilings, period features including open fires, combined with luxurious fittings and high-tech installations like surround sound throughout and a top of the range media system, plus a fully equipped gym, make this house perfect for me.

"Thanks, Bob. I've had a long drive, so I'll sign all the paperwork tomorrow and drop it to your office." Turning to face him once more I add, "So if you don't mind, I'd like to get settled in."

"Of course, of course. I'll leave you to it." He holds his hand out for me to shake and I offer him mine while steering him towards the front door.

"If you need anything, I've left our office number and my direct number on the counter in the kitchen. Call anytime."

"Thanks again, Bob." I open the door while keeping my polite smile in place until Bob is left standing alone on the pavement outside and I'm finally alone.

This is it.

A fresh start.

I don't bother unpacking. Instead, I grab a bottle of beer from my fully stocked fridge- thanks, Bob- sprawl on my new sofa and flick on the television. Propping my feet on the low coffee table, I take a long draw from my bottle and select a random film.

Everything feels different but good.

New, but exciting.

I'm alone in a new city without Lei as my crutch, and for the first time in a long time, I feel alive and ready for what's to come.

With a few days free until I have to report for costume

fittings ready for filming, I plan out in my head the places I want to visit while I'm here.

First things first, tomorrow I'll unpack then I'm heading straight to the Doctor Who Experience in Cardiff Bay.

Don't judge me. We are all big kids at heart, and I've been a Whovian since the day I found out my brother was scared of Daleks.

It was a Saturday night tradition at our house to watch the show together and Clark- yes, I can say his name now without choking- would sit and hide behind a cushion for the entire episode. So I'm visiting the exhibit for him as much as me. I want to begin to remember the good things and not the bad. I want my brother back; I want his memories back. I'm ready to forgive him.

In fact, I think I already have.

With another long drink of beer, I sigh contently and close my eyes.

"To new beginnings."

# chapter 13

*Isaac*

**F**uck. I miss them.

Seeing Ivy's little face on the screen before me while we *FaceTime* only serves to heighten this feeling.

"We're going to the beach, Uncle Iz."

Her cherubic face framed in blonde ringlets is so reminiscent of her mother's, but while she has her mother's looks she has her father's shy disposition.

I grin big at her excitement, my smile hiding the concerns I have about Josh taking his kids away from everyone they know and love to spend the summer in Ibiza.

"I know, your Daddy told me. I bet you can't wait to swim in the sea and make sandcastles on the beach. You're going to have so much fun."

She nods enthusiastically, flashing me her pearly milk

teeth with a wide smile.

"Yep. I'm a big girl so I can build one all by myself, but Arthur is too little so Daddy said I must help him."

I love the way she pronounces Arthur- *Arfurr-* Josh stuck with the name Laura wanted for their little one despite their numerous disagreements before he was born. The name suits the bouncing baby boy, and it was Laura's grandfather's name, so it's fitting that he bears the family moniker that his mother wanted.

"Your Dad is right, you need to look after your little brother, he needs his big sister to look out for him."

*And so does your Daddy. He needs you even though your young shoulders shouldn't have to bear that weight.*

"Are you coming with us?" Her bright eyes shine out from the screen in front of me, and my heart lurches. It's the same question she's asked me almost every day for the last few weeks. As soon as she found out they were going she expected me to tag along with them. Telling her no is one of the hardest things I've ever had to do, but my mother is right, Josh needs to do this on his own. It's time for him to be a fully functioning father again and not a robotic droid who is unable to emotionally invest himself in his children's lives.

"No, Ivy-Leaves. I can't come with you. I have to work, remember?"

Her bottom lip wobbles and I'm seconds away from taking those words back, calling Jake and telling him to give my job to someone else.

Just as I open my mouth to say just that, Josh's face comes

into view.

"Come on, Ivy. We've talked about this. Uncle Iz can't stay with us forever. He's got a life of his own to get on with. Now say goodbye and then go and clean your teeth ready for bed. I'll be up to tuck you in soon."

"Can Uncle Iz read me a bedtime story?"

Her little face turns to mine once more but before I can reply Josh's stern voice chastises her. "Ivy, enough. Go and do as you're told. Uncle Iz is away with his work. He's not reading you a story. Now get up those stairs and brush your teeth."

Tears spill over her long lashes and roll down her pink cheeks. *Fuck.* I knew that leaving them wasn't a good idea. He's not ready for this; they need me.

"I can…" I begin, about to offer to read to her over *FaceTime.*

"*No!* Stop, Isaac. She needs to listen to me. I'm her Dad, and I say it's bedtime." His eyes flash with anger behind his thick-framed glasses, and I'm seconds away from getting on my bike and riding back to London whether he likes it or not.

"G-g-g-night Uncle Iz. I love you."

Ivy's sweet face struggles to hold back her emotions, and she bravely blows me a kiss before jumping down from the sofa and disappearing from my screen.

When I think she's gone and can't hear me, I let loose.

"Josh, there was no need to get angry with her. She's too young to understand all these changes. First I leave, when

I've been a huge part of her life for the last year, then you decide to take them away to another country…"

"Butt out, Iz. I appreciate everything you've done for us but do not tell me how to raise my kids."

His eyes bore into mine through my tablet screen. Anger and annoyance evident in his features.

"I'm not telling you anything. I'm just saying she's not even three years old and she's struggling too, Josh. You can't expect…"

"*Stop!*"

He tears his glasses off and runs his hand over his face before pinching the bridge of his nose.

"You think I don't know all this? You think I don't know what a shitty father I am?" He laughs sardonically, "I know what a piss-poor excuse for a parent I've been the last year. I fucking know. I don't need you ramming it down my throat or trying to take my place."

Is that what he thinks I've been doing?

"I'm not, I wasn't trying to…"

"Listen, I'm grateful, I really am, but this is why I'm taking the kids away. It'll be good for us. There're too many reminders here, and I just want to do what's best for them and right now staying here is killing me. Sleeping in the same bed, sitting on the same sofa, drinking out of the same mugs, even tucking Ivy up in the same sheets, is too much. It's all the same here. It's all Laura. She's everywhere and yet nowhere. Everything I see, everything I touch, everything I smell is a reminder of her not being here with us. I feel like I'm living in an alternate reality. I can't function another second in this house with all our things surrounding me." He shakes his head, defeat, grief and sadness emanating from his features. "It's all still here but she's not, and it's wrong, Iz. It's so fucking wrong that I can't breathe for feeling her but not touching her, for smelling her, but not seeing her. I need out, and I won't ever be coming back to this place."

His shoulders slump. His outpouring of words a clear manifestation of the grief that still consumes him. I don't know what to say. What worthless combination of vowels and consonants can I form to make any of this any better?

"I'm here for you."

His weary eyes blink at me from the screen. His defeated facade made all the more heart-breaking by the small smile he attempts to form.

"I know. Iz."

We stare at each other in silence. Josh's face trying to convey that he's going to be okay, and mine attempting to show him that even in silence I'm not going anywhere. If he needs me, I'll be there.

"Go on now, big shot movie maker. Go and show our hotshot brother that he's not the only one with silver screen talent."

I quietly laugh and shake my head. "I'm not acting in Jake's film. I'm doing the cinematography."

"Yeah, whatever. Just go and show Jake how it's done before his head gets too big for his megastar shoulders."

We both laugh at that. Jake may once have been a cocky

bastard but Emma changed all that, he's not at all showy of his success and fame.

"Okay, I will do. But if you need…"

"I won't, Iz. But thank you. I'll make sure to give Ivy a kiss from her favourite uncle. We'll give you a call when we get to Ibiza."

"Alright, bro. I'll speak to you soon. Give Arty a kiss from me too."

"His name is Arthur."

"Yeah, but he likes Arty."

"He's not even one yet. He doesn't know what he likes."

"Yeah, he does. He's a bright boy."

A sad smile graces Josh's face, and I know just what he's thinking because I'm thinking the same. He's just like his Mum.

"Speak soon, bro."

He doesn't wait for my goodbye. He disconnects *FaceTime* without making eye contact again, and I find myself staring at my troubled reflection in the black screen before me.

After a crappy night's sleep where I worried constantly about Josh and the kids, I drag myself out of bed at the arse crack of dawn and find myself in the unfamiliar kitchen of my new rented home.

I'm two doors down from Jake and his family and a few doors away from a couple of the actors who are starring in my brother's first ever feature film. Well, it's not his first movie, but it's his first as a director, and I know he wants to make it a huge success.

I grab a protein shake from the fridge- the estate agent helpfully stocked the house with all my requirements before I got here- slip on my running shoes and head out into the cool early morning air for my usual ten-mile run.

I'm hardly what you could call an overly athletic or sporty person, but I like running. No skill is required to be able to do it, and it's great therapy. It also helps me maintain a body that both the chicks and guys seem to like. What can I say? I have a healthy libido or I should say I *had* a healthy libido. There hasn't been anyone for almost a year. I've spent the last twelve months with Josh and his kids. They needed me, and that left me zero time for any nocturnal activities.

The last time I got intimate with anyone was... *Flynn Phillips*. Yeah, that worked out well. Okay, so it wasn't just Flynn that night, Céline was a part of it too, although I can only remember Flynn. I recall everything about him, from his cut body to the worn leather bracelet on his wrist, which is a little worrying considering how that night ended.

I wonder what he's doing now? I wonder if he's finally sorted his head out because bloody hell did he have some major issues.

Issues that made him lash out at me in the ugliest way possible.

I don't hold it against him, though. He's a really cool guy if you take away his denial. Plus, we all have baggage. Who am I to judge anyone? It took me long enough to accept that I am who I am and I love who I love. Not that I've ever been in love. Lust? Yes. Love? That word only brings heartache and loss. Just look at Josh. Give me lust over love anytime.

My feet pound the pavement as I weave my way through the suburban streets towards Pontcanna Fields. I asked the estate agent the nearest place to go running, and he recommended this leafy park just a short jog from my new house. When I approach the entrance, I hit my running playlist on my phone, crank up the volume and pick up my pace to the sounds of indie rock blaring through my earphones.

Bob, the estate agent, was right. This is a great place for a run; flat, green and with a stunning view of the River Taff. Friendlier than London too as I pass by many walkers, cyclists and joggers who all give a smile as they go on their way.

I'm approaching mile four when my eyes land on another jogger up ahead running towards me. Tall, wearing low-slung shorts, a tight vest and bright blue running shoes, his long legs eat up the ground with his powerful stride. The closer we get the more of him I can make out. He has messy dark hair, a cool set of *Bose* headphones on his ears and a body that has seen many hours in the gym. We are just a few strides away from each other when our eyes clash and my stomach bottoms out causing me to stumble and lose my stride. I correct myself just in time to gawp, open mouthed like a fucking fish floundering for air on an arid riverbank. Recognition flashes over his face as he too stumbles but manages to pick up his pace in time to run past me fluidly, his eyes never leaving mine until he's passed by and is sprinting off in the opposite direction.

Flynn fucking Phillips is in Cardiff.

It's as if I thought of him and he materialised in front of me. Like just remembering the last night I saw him has somehow conjured him up out of thin air.

Slowing down, I turn and jog backwards to enable myself to watch him run away. I need another visual confirmation that my eyes aren't playing tricks on me and that the stunningly sexy man who just ran past me is indeed Flynn.

His back is stiff, his strides purposeful and I can't help but drop my eyes to his perfectly shaped arse that is made all the more mouth-watering by the tight fabric skimming over those perfect glutes.

I flick my eyes back up in time to see him look over his shoulder and stumble again.

*Fuck me.*

It is him.

The last man I saw naked. The man whose ripped body is imprinted on my brain. The man whose image I've wanked off to far too many times to count over the last year.

What the hell is he doing here?

I guess I'm about to find out because the man I am shamelessly staring at while jogging backwards has just turned and is heading straight for me.

Flynn fucking Phillips is running right at me, sweat causing his tight top to cling to his muscles, exertion flushing his cheeks red, making him even hotter than I can remember.

He's my every wet dream in the flesh. He's also my every nightmare, and he's gaining on me with every purposeful stride of his long, muscled legs.

I swear to God I may just hyperventilate.

This cannot be real life, someone with a camera is going to jump out of the bushes and scream 'You've been punked' any second now.

Three- his eyes are locked on mine.

Two- his full lips tip up into a nervous smile.

One- "Isaac? I thought it was you."

Zero.

# chapter 14

*Flynn*

I am so in the zone that the reality of seeing Isaac right in front of me takes a moment to register through my surprise.

I could've done my morning run in my new place. The fully equipped gym has a top of the range running machine, and I initially planned to make good use of it, but with the sun breaking out over the horizon and the early morning air crisp against my overheated skin, I knew I'd made the right decision to check out the local area. That is until I come face-to-face with the man I've tried to eradicate from my memories.

It was his eyes I noticed first, even from many feet away I felt their intense stare. When I looked directly at the face that held those eyes, recognition wasn't immediate. He looked like Isaac, and my body felt the same reaction it always does to his presence, but he was different.

Gone was his shoulder length hair to be replaced by a messy style that was short on the sides and longer on top. His strong, defined jaw led to his full mouth and fat bottom lip. A jaw that I remembered was previously hidden beneath a cascade of waves that somewhat softened his chiselled features. Now, he looks even more masculine, even more manly and if my cock has any say in the matter, even more attractive. I'm not sure if it's shock or his new appearance or a combination of both, but my mind can't quite grasp that the man who just ran past me is *him,* Isaac Fox.

Even after passing him I feel his stare and my head turns of its own accord to double check, my heart frantically beating in my chest and not because of the twelve miles I'd already run.

When I look over my shoulder, sure enough, he's slowly jogging backwards and staring at me, or at this precise moment in time he's staring at my arse. Why does that shoot a thrill down my spine that settles firmly in my heavy balls?

*Keep running. Do not turn back.*

Only every single part of me begs to turn back.

My therapist suggested that moving on would be easier for me if I made amends with the people that I felt I had done wrong.

Isaac is one of those people. The things I said to him, *about him,* were unforgivable. Maybe this is my chance to make that right? Maybe I'm being given the perfect opportunity to do the right thing and begin my fresh start with a clean slate.

*Maybe.*

Before I can talk myself out of it, I turn on the spot and sprint back in his direction. He's still jogging backwards but appears to be about to turn around, until he sees me heading his way. Then his mouth drops open, and he gapes, yes, gapes, as if he can't really believe that I would want to talk to him or more likely that I have the audacity to think he wants to talk to me.

"Isaac? I thought it was you."

*Smooth, Flynn. Real fucking smooth.*

Silence.

He's still staring at me like I have three heads and man boobs.

"I, uh… what are you doing here?"

*Still with the smoothness.*

His mouth closes and opens a few times, but he remains jogging on the spot while I stand stock still, hands on my hips waiting for a reply like an idiot.

"Sorry, this was stupid of me. I guess I…" I'm about to ramble some shit about leaving when he shocks the crap out of me and interrupts.

"I have a few miles left to go, but do you fancy grabbing a coffee in say an hour? I saw a great looking breakfast place just down the road."

He looks nervous. His typically cool, calm and relaxed demeanour is nowhere to be seen and it only serves to make him even more attractive. I make him nervous. That's a good thing, right? It's better than out and out anger or hate which is no less than I deserve.

"Yeah, sure. Coffee sounds great," I reply while fidgeting with the leather strap around my wrist.

*Coffee sounds great? Wow, I'm killing this conversation.*

Just like that, Isaac's nerves disappear, and his stance becomes more confident. His wide lips stretch into a charming grin, and my cock appreciates the view of his stubbled jaw as it moves.

*Yeah, it's still him that does this to me. Only him.*

"Cool. I'll be done in around an hour. I'll meet you there for eight. The place is called *Brava*. I'll have an *Americano*."

Cocky, he's already placing his coffee order, and again it just makes him more appealing. Is there anything that could make this guy a turn-off for me?

"I guess coffee is on me then. I'll see you at eight."

He nods and gives me a shit-eating grin then turns and sprints away.

I watch, of course, until he becomes a speck in the distance and I realise I'm standing in the middle of a busy park, with runners and cyclists whizzing past me, a matching shit-eating smile on my face.

I stretch out my now stiff muscles, my legs protesting at the lack of cool down and jog back to my new place to grab a quick shower.

I don't want to make it look like I changed just for him, so I pull on some sports bottoms and a hoody, quickly style my hair, making sure to make it look like I haven't bothered too much and make my way to the café he mentioned.

It's a five-minute walk away and even this early in the morning it's bustling with people grabbing their morning java.

I check the time as I walk through the doors and see that I have ten minutes to order and grab us a seat.

Selecting a table that faces the door, I grab our coffees, including his requested *Americano* and add a couple of bran muffins and pastries.

I'm starving so he's sure to be, it has nothing to do with wanting to please him. I need food, so he likely does too.

My knee bounces under the table, and I readjust my seat about a dozen times trying to get comfortable.

What am I going to say to him? Sorry is hardly going to cut it, and I *do not* want to go into detail about my pathetic issues or talk about my brother. Maybe he's coming here to give me a piece of his mind? Maybe he won't turn up and I'll be stood up? Yeah, like this is a date.

*This is not a date.*

Just as I'm forcing my body to recline casually in my chair, he strides through the door. His skin flushed from his run, and his hair slicked back against his head in messy waves like he's been running his fingers through the sweaty strands.

Why is that so hot to me?

I'm not just nervous. I'm on pins. My nerves are jangling through my body, and my heart is pounding in my chest.

He's just a guy I need to make amends with, and he can either accept my apology or walk away. That's all I'm here for, nothing else.

*Keep telling yourself that.*

"You came."

"You're here."

*I guess we both thought we were going to be stood up.*

We laugh awkwardly at our similar greetings and Isaac takes a seat opposite me, his long legs stretching out under the table bracketing mine but not touching. His intense eyes take in every inch of my face, and despite his laid-back appearance, I can tell he's still shocked to be here with me.

"So, how come you're in Cardiff? You have a book tour going on?"

He picks up his drink and helps himself to a muffin from the tray. His question is easy to answer and an obvious conversation starter. I appreciate the fact he's going easy on me.

"Nah. I'm taking a break from that side of the business. Elaina, my PA, has helped me employ a management team to take over the fitness plan sign-ups and I've fulfilled my publishing contract for three books. I'm here to try something else."

He finishes chewing his bite of food and washes it down with a gulp of coffee before speaking. "It's always good to try something new."

That's quite a closed response. Where should I take the conversation now? Go straight into an apology? Lucky for me, he gives me another break and asks, "So are you here for a few days or longer?"

"I'm renting a place not far from here. I'll be in Cardiff for at least six months. I may even decide to stay and continue working from here. How about you? You have a shoot in Wales or…?"

"I'm working for my brother. I haven't taken on any new projects for a while, and he offered me this opportunity. The timing was perfect, so I'll be here for a few months too."

The penny drops.

Jake Fox. Isaac Fox.

Brothers.

I'm working with his brother on this new film, and Isaac is working with him… on his new film.

*Fuck.* Things could get awkward. So much for new beginnings. I need to get this apology out and try and make both our lives a little less uncomfortable.

Shifting in my seat, I lean forward to pick up my coffee, then think better of it and take back my hand, sliding it under my thigh instead. I can't be trusted not to wave my arms around while I ramble, so it's better if I sit on them than look like a complete nob.

"I'm, uh… I need to… uh. What I'm trying to say is…"

"It's okay."

I lift my anxious gaze from the table top to look at his face. Those two words are spoken with such compassion and understanding that I struggle to blink for a second and can only stare.

# one

His face is honest and open, his body language calm and inviting and as much as I want to accept how graciously he's letting me off the hook, I don't deserve it, and he deserves more.

"No. Listen. It's not okay. I turned back to talk to you today instead of running away because I need to apologise, in fact, I need to do more than that, but at least it's a start." I sit straighter in my seat and make sure to maintain eye contact, even when my entire body screams at me to look away from the one person I can't ever seem to purge from my mind.

"My reaction, the things I said to you, I don't have an excuse. Well, I don't have a good enough excuse. I've been through some...um, stuff, but that's not on you, that's all me and those hateful things I said, although I directed them at you, they weren't because of you. I wish I could take them away and pretend I never said them, but I can't so all I have to offer are new words, words of apology that I hope you don't find meaningless because I couldn't mean them more."

I break our stare and look out into the sunny street. My tongue trips over words, wanting to find ones that mean something and I only come up with one. *Sorry.*

Turning my head to face him once more and locking my eyes with his intense hazel gaze I speak two simple words from the heart and hope he can feel the truth of them.

"I'm sorry."

"I forgive you."

His smile is small but genuine, his eyes full of the

forgiveness he spoke.

"It's not as simple as that."

"It's as simple as we want it to be," he counters quickly. "Life is too short, Flynn. Live it without regrets."

His hand extends across the table and rests flat on the surface in front of me. "If you get a chance, take it. If it changes your life for the better, let it. If it's worth the risk, then gamble because happiness can be fucking fleeting and forgiveness can be given and accepted easily without the burden of grudges. I've accepted your apology. Can you accept my forgiveness?"

*C*an you accept my forgiveness?

I stand before the outfit worn by *David Tennant*, the tenth *Doctor Who*, but I don't actually see it. I mean, of course I see it, but my head just keeps repeating my encounter with Isaac on a fucking loop. It's like being stuck on a bad rerun of an angsty chick-flick. Only I'm not *Ryan Reynolds*; I'm his snivelling, over-thinking co-star. Damn it all to hell. Why can't I be *Ryan Reynolds*?

"I preferred *Tom Baker*. He liked *Jelly Beans* just like me."

A small voice breaks into my internal replay of Isaac's forgiveness monologue, and I turn my head to the side to see a young lad of about ten or eleven staring at a costume that was worn by *Billie Piper* when she played the Doctor's sidekick, Rose.

He doesn't turn to look at me but keeps rattling off facts

and opinions on everything from *Doctor Who* baddies to the new improved *Tardis* and why it is blasphemy that *Torchwood* got canned.

"I take it you're a fan?" I tease when he finally breaks for air. Turning his head slowly to give me a 'Duh' face, I'm struck by how much this boy reminds me of my brother Clark.

With a mop of messy auburn curls that could do with a good trim, pale freckled skin and big blue eyes, this boy could well be his son, if he'd ever had one. The uncanny resemblance may have once sent me running away unable to face the memories of my brother, but between months of therapy and the fact that I bump into this kid here, at the *Doctor Who Experience,* of all places, kind of feels like serendipity.

"Would I be here if I wasn't?" he asks a little confused.

Fair enough.

I smile and shrug in return, but then he asks, "Are you a fan?"

"Would I be here if I wasn't?" I toss back and then add for good measure, "Besides, everyone knows Tennant is the ultimate Doctor, it's a fact."

"Whatever." Is the typical kid response received.

I chuckle under my breath and turn around to find out who he's with. The kid must understand what I'm doing because he says, "I've got a season pass, I come here all the time. My mum will pick me up outside when I'm done."

"That's cool," I reply because I have nothing else to say

and wonder why I'm still talking to this random kid that kinda looks like a young version of my dead brother.

"Okay, nice chatting with you, *Bakerite,* but I've gotta head off now, adult things to do and all that."

"It's Clarke."

I'm about to turn but stop dead. My throat closes up restricting the air getting to my lungs, and my stomach plummets until I feel it hit the floor with a reverberating thud.

Slowly I turn to face the boy. "What did you say?"

He tears his gaze away from a costume that I now know he must have studied hundreds of times before and slowly speaks like I'm an imbecile and he needs to make me understand. "My name, it's Clarke. C-L-A-R…"

"K." I finish for him, the letter coming out with a rasp as though the sound tore at the flesh of my throat before exploding into the air.

"E," he tags on, oblivious to my struggle.

"C-L-A-R-K-E, Clarke with an E. My mum wanted me to have her maiden name so gave it to me as my first name. Kind of geeky, hey."

I can feel the blood rushing out of my head and pooling somewhere on the floor leaving my brain starved of oxygen. I bend over at the waist and grip my knees, like a man that has just run a marathon and needs to catch his breath.

"You okay, Mister? You're not looking so good."

I lift my head enough to look him in the face, his familiar, freckled face that isn't my brother.

## one

"I'm good. I just thought you were going to say like *Clark Gable*. I knew someone once who was named after him because his mother liked old time movie stars. He had a brother called Flynn, named after *Errol Flynn*." I'm breathlessly rambling to a young lad who hasn't got a clue what I'm talking about.

Scratching his head, he gives me a once over to make sure I'm not going to keel over and says, "Cool. Wanna come to the gift shop and check out their new stock?"

I huff out an unexpected laugh at the weirdness of this whole situation, and it's enough to clear the fog from my brain and allow me to stand up without falling flat on my arse after my ridiculous little panic attack.

"Sure, kid." I run my hand over my face and then motion him forward with my extended arm, "Lead the way."

An hour and around seventy quid later, Clarke with an E leaves the building to meet his mother with an Airfix model set of the *Tardis* he told me he's been coveting for over a year and a few other random items. I left with a keyring and a weird sense of rightness after spending time with a kid that may have looked like my brother but was actually nothing like him, despite their shared moniker.

I'm guessing he's going to have a hard time explaining why some random stranger bought him so much stuff and maybe I should be worried about being accused of grooming or some weird shit, but that kid gave me something precious today that I haven't had in a long time. Fun, happiness and in a strange way, acceptance.

I wasn't famous to him, he had zero expectations of who I am or who I'm supposed to be, I was just Flynn, his new mate.

I haven't felt this light for a long time, if ever.

Maybe it's time I focused on who I am and who I want to be, not who I think I should be.

Here's to Clarke with an E.

No more ghosts, no more whys or what ifs, no more blaming, no more hating and no more expectations or ridiculous notions that my brother killed himself because of his hidden sexuality.

It was more than that.

He was more than that.

And so am I.

# chapter 15

*Isaac*

The first day on location is chaotic.

Having spent the last few days checking out all the local areas I'd previously scouted for the initial days of filming, now was the time to bring Jake's vision to life. But first, I needed to meet the cast and crew. It was all good and well to know the scenery and the logistics of making this shoot work, but I needed to meet the people who would bring it all to life.

I knew Jake had, against all professional advice, hired a cast of relative unknowns, but I hadn't yet asked who they are or even bothered to research cast members. Yeah, slacking in the preparation department again and it reminds me of the last time I was caught short on a shoot and came face to face with... Flynn fucking Phillips.

I'm not even joking right now.

Flynn Phillips is right in front of me.

He may have a freshly shaved head, a face full of impressively realistic prosthetics and a lethal looking hunting knife flipping through his nimble fingers but I can tell that man apart from any other person in the entire world.

And he's sitting not five feet in front of me getting last minute touches to his makeup.

Almost as if he senses my arrival, his head lifts and those soulful brown eyes meet mine, instantly crinkling at the corners as his deliciously plump mouth tilts up in a warm and welcoming smile.

*Fuck me.* This man is devastating.

Without realising it, I've matched his smile and my feet, having a mind of their own, have moved me so that I now stand directly in front of him.

"Hey," his hand lifts and he motions to his bald head and scarred face, "I thought I'd be unrecognisable looking like this."

He's made it too easy.

"Sorry, who are you? I'm looking for the actor playing a character called…" I glance down at the sheaf of notes in my hand pretending to scan the list of names before looking back at his freakily sexy face, "Grim. You must be him."

His face falters for a second before he notices the slight quirk of my lips that I can't control because he totally fell for my lame attempt at teasing.

Extending his hand to me he says, "That's me, Flynn

Phillips. Pleased to meet you and you are?"

*Funny fucker.*

That's okay. I can play along with him a while longer.

Grasping his large hand in mine, I have to stifle the shudder that runs through me when our skin touches, almost like a current of energy passes from him into me and hits me right in the chest.

"Isaac Fox, but please, call me Iz. All my friends and lovers do."

*Take that.* If anything is certain to get a reaction, it will be that overly suggestive comment. Only it backfires. Flynn's grin widens as he looks from the oblivious makeup artist, who is concentrating on dusting down his smoothly shaven head and is ignorant to our exchange and the electricity that is so tangible it practically crackles in the air around us, back to me.

"I guess I'll call you Iz, then." He squeezes my hand as the one syllable of my nickname leaves his lips but instead of letting go he holds firm.

Well isn't this a surprise. Gone is the uptight, closeted homophobe only to be replaced by the relaxed and dare I say flirty man before me.

And fuck if it doesn't make him even more irresistible.

Coughing to clear my throat, I slowly extract my hand from his. Not because I want to but because if I don't I may shut his cocky mouth with my tongue.

I've practically been a freaking monk for the last twelve months, and this unexpected interaction has me just about fit to burst.

"Well… *Flynn Phillips,* it was great to meet you. Enjoy the first day of filming. Hopefully, I'll catch you around."

*Soon my lips ache to say. Really fucking soon.*

"How about tonight? I only have a few hours on set today. I could use a new *friend.*"

Is it me or did the way he said *friend* sound more like *lover?*

Needing to regain some composure, I take a step backwards and answer as relaxed as possible despite the raging boner in my jeans, "Sure. There's a pub not far from my place called *The Cricketers.* I'll be there around nine once I finish up here."

I'm steadily inching backwards probably trying and failing to dampen down my obvious enthusiasm.

"I've seen the place. Look forward to it. See you at nine."

He gives me one last dick-hardening smile and doesn't break our gaze until I turn and walk away. Even then I can feel his eyes on me until I round the corner out of sight.

Who is that man and what has he done with Flynn Phillips?

After a long but invigorating first day, I head back to my place with a spring in my step. One that my brother Jake doesn't miss and happily brings up as soon as we are out of earshot.

"Okay, so which one of my production assistants are you

shagging or planning to shag? Please tell me it's not Callie? She's cute but fresh out of college, and too bloody young and innocent for the likes of you, plus she's good at her job and I'd like to keep her around."

He's driving us back home as our rental houses are on the same street just a couple of doors apart.

"Why do you assume I'm shagging anyone? It was a good first day and I'm excited to be back in work. Isn't that enough of an explanation?"

He takes his eyes off the road to glance quickly in my direction, his face saying everything he's also about to say with words.

"For anyone else, yes. For you, no. So spill it. Who do I have to keep an eye on when you fuck them and leave them wanting more? The ramifications will probably throw my whole production schedule into chaos."

He's only semi-joking, his tone of voice betraying his concern.

"For fuck's sake, Jake. I can keep it in my pants. You don't need to judge everyone on how you used to be before Emma made you an honest man."

"This film…"

I don't let him finish. He's way off base with his theory. Well, he's slightly off base at the very least.

"Is important to you. Your baby." I stare at his profile now highlighted with the fading evening sun. "I'm a professional, Jake. I've managed to keep my cock in my pants for almost a year while I was with Josh and the kids, so I think I can keep the beast tamed a little while longer, don't you?"

"Fair enough, but something has got you all giddy like a schoolgirl attending her first boy band concert."

I laugh at that. He's not far wrong. My nerves are jangling and tingling so hard when I think about meeting Flynn tonight that I can almost hear them buzzing across my skin.

"I'm just fired up about the film. It's a new challenge and I'm getting to do something I love again after being Uncle Iz, bum-changer, dribble-cleaner and bedtime story reader extraordinaire for so long that I almost forget I'm a single, professional man with aspirations above what to watch on *Netflix* when the kids are finally asleep."

That makes him laugh. Having a child of his own means he can fully appreciate everything I've just said.

"I hope Josh will be okay in Ibiza," I wonder softly.

His laughter dies and he instantly becomes more sombre. "Yeah, me too. I think Mum said something about going out there for a few weeks, but Dad doesn't think it's a good idea. Part of me agrees with him because Josh needs to learn to live again for himself and his family, but the other part of me worries he's not ready for it."

"He's not." It's the truth. My gut twists with concern for my brother and his children and I daily have to talk myself out of jumping on a plane and going to check on them, but I have to trust his judgment and hope this is the thing that will make him not break him further.

"But Dad's right. It's time for him to live, the kids need him, and not the husk of a man he's become. Laura wouldn't have wanted this for him, and that's what hurts the most. He just can't see it. He's still so deep in his grief that nothing I said could get through to him."

Jake swallows down the words he was about to add and silence claims us. Both of us are caught up in our thoughts and worries until thirty minutes later we pull up outside my house.

"Thanks for the ride home, bro. I'll take the bike in tomorrow. I want to get an early start on the set up of that empty property we are using for the Billy Williams scene."

Talking about filming breaks through the melancholy that blanketed the final half of our ride home.

"Yeah, tomorrow should be fun. It's the start of the blood bath. I can't wait to see it all come to life." He grins like a kid in a sweet shop.

I open the door and step out onto the kerb then lean into the car through the opening.

"I'm gonna grab a pint in the pub down the road if you fancy it?"

*Why the fuck am I inviting Jake? Please say no, please say no.*

"I'll pass. I've missed the fuck out of Emmy and CJ. It's great having them here with me, so I want to make the most of coming home to them regularly. That's the perks of filming in the U.K. for a change."

"Don't blame you, bro. Say hi from me and tell Caleb I'll be over to play with his new cars sometime this week."

"Will do. Enjoy your date tonight."

I'm about to slam the door when he throws that out there, and I stare at him like a shell-shocked idiot only confirming his suspicions.

"Ha! I fucking knew it. It better not be one of my crew is all I'm saying and make sure to wrap it up. You've just played surrogate Daddy for the last few months. You don't want to land yourself with your own mini-me."

I shake my head and slam the door, leaning in through the open window to say, "Thanks for the pep talk, Mum."

All the cocky bastard does is grin before pulling away and stopping a couple of doors down the street, throwing me a salute as he walks out of sight towards his front door.

*Wrap it up.*

If only he knew who I was meeting in an hour's time, his warning would be a little different. It would be more like 'Stay the fuck away.'

Yeah, tried that and failed.

When Flynn is around, it's an impossible task.

*L*ess than an hour later I walk into *The Cricketers* pub and immediately zone in on the broad back of the man at the bar.

It's not the way his shirt pulls tightly across his wide shoulders or the way his newly shaved head begs for my hands to smooth themselves over the recently exposed skin that makes me ache for the man before me. It's the way his foot nervously bounces on the rung of the barstool as he tries to pay attention to the busty blonde who is doing her damnedest to get into his pants and failing miserably.

His leg bounces because of me.

He ignores the blatant advances of a hot woman because of me.

His back straightens when he feels my presence behind him, because of me.

And fuck if it doesn't feel good.

How many more reactions can I get out of him tonight that solely belong to me?

I can't fucking wait to find out.

# chapter 16

## *Flynn*

Just like every other time Isaac Fox has walked into the room I'm in, I feel him before I even see him.

It's like his essence floods the air and lands directly on the invisible 'Isaac only' receptors on my skin.

I've never experienced this with anyone else before in my entire life. Only him.

Always him.

I can't even begin to understand it. This tangible link we have. It makes no sense; it's stronger than attraction, and it messes with my head because he's a man.

I'm not in denial. I'm not lying to myself. The effect he has on me is unique to him and him alone. It's the Isaac Effect. A phenomenon I cannot even come close to explaining or understanding. It just is.

# *one*

He slips onto the barstool beside me, and the slight brush of his leg against mine reverberates through my entire body.

His touch is so fucking potent that I have to physically remind myself to breathe.

"You look good without hair." The words whisper in my ear before he leans back on his stool and instantly grabs the attention of the barmaid who had been trying quite unsuccessfully to engage me in a conversation for the last fifteen or so minutes. I don't blame her for noticing him, he's hard to miss.

I self-consciously rub my hand over my freshly shorn head and turn to meet his gaze. "And you look good with short hair."

My eyes flick over his new hairstyle before landing back on his face, and this time it's he who looks uncharacteristically self-conscious.

"Yeah, I fancied a change. I'm still not used to it. I keep trying to tuck the strands behind my ear. Old habits die hard."

"Change is as good as a rest, or so they say." I smile and take a sip of my beer.

"I think that applies to your occupation, not a new hairstyle."

"Well, then that works too, seeing as we are both starting out on a new path. Talking of which, how did your first day on set go?"

Isaac thanks the barmaid and dismisses her flirty smile by turning to face me fully.

"Invigorating. How about you? Must be different playing

a whole new person on screen and not yourself?"

I shrug, knocking back some more of my drink. "Who said that's not what I've been doing for the last few years anyway? Doesn't everyone play a role in life?"

Fuck, this light-hearted conversation is turning a little deep fast.

"Not me, what you see is what you get. I'm too old for playing games." He smirks at me in an attempt to lighten the mood, his entire body facing mine, his attention firmly on my face as if there is no one else in the room. The intensity of his gaze is something that has always put me off balance despite the thrill of earning a man like Isaac's attentiveness.

"So," he continues. "What does it feel like to play a blood thirsty killer with more 'Mommy issues' than the bloke in *Psycho*? Some of the shit you have to film tomorrow looks gory as fuck."

Setting my pint on the bar top, I twist my body to mirror his pose and reply, "Surprisingly cathartic. I mean, what better way to break out from being Flynn Phillips the body, than to become a man with more scars inside than he has on the outside? And you've seen the prosthetics. He's pretty fucked up. Plus," I lean forward conspiratorially lowering my voice to whisper, "I've learned how to dismember and hide a body so if anyone ever messes with me in the future…" I waggle my eyebrows for effect, probably looking more like a pleb than a killer.

"Duly noted." He laughs and turns back towards his pint. I watch the way his throat bobs with each swallow as he takes a long drink and when he angles his eyes to look at me and raises a brow before using his thumb to wipe froth from his upper lip, I realise I've been caught staring.

Needing to break this weird connection I rush out, "So what have you been up to the last year? I haven't seen any new stuff from you." Recognising that I'm admitting to knowing this information about him, I quickly add, "Not that I've researched or been looking, I mean I just…"

He chuckles and I nervously stop rambling and pick up my pint to give my hands and my mouth something to do besides digging me into a deeper hole.

"I took a year out. Family stuff."

Huh. That's all I'm gonna get? Fair enough.

"What about you? I saw how many companies were vying for you to endorse their products after that *Wicked Water* advert. Is it true you turned down an *Armani* campaign?"

The smile on his face lets me know that he's openly admitted to following news on me for the last few months and I'm not just flattered, I'm confused.

Why would a man like Isaac, one who I attacked in the worst way possible, one that can have practically anyone he wants to jump in his bed, admit to following my career over the last twelve months?

"I uh, I wasn't interested in continuing to be known just for my body. I wanted to change my career path and despite it being a great opportunity and a huge amount of money, it wasn't what I wanted or needed at that time."

"I get that." His eyes connect and hold with mine, "And

for the record, as amazing as your body is, I've always seen you as more than that."

The air around us thickens. He's making his intentions known and now is the time for me to succumb to it or end it once and for all.

"I want to get to know you, Flynn."

His words snap me out of my internal war, and I once more lift my eyes to his intense hazel stare.

"I'm not going to lie and say I don't want you in my bed, but for whatever reason," he laughs to himself and shakes his head before once more ensnaring me with his gaze, "I want to get to know you more. I could use a friend, I'm guessing you could too, so how about it?"

He holds out his hand to me, and I drag my eyes from his face to look at his gesture of friendship.

He's right. I've been pretty closed off, only allowing Elaina into my inner circle, but could we ever just be friends?

My head lifts to his open and honest face. His ridiculously attractive face, and the decision is easy. He's giving me a second chance, and I'm taking it with both hands.

So that's what I do. I turn and fully enclosed Isaac's large, warm hand between both of mine, giving it a firm shake.

"Friends sounds good."

My agreement sets off a chain reaction.

His face breaks out into a genuinely happy grin, and a bolt of electricity passes between our joined hands at the touch of his skin on mine and the open joy on his face.

"Let's drink to that. I spotted a pool table in the next

room. What say we seal this friendship with a tournament? Winner pays for the drinks."

"Deal. But get your wallet ready. I'm playing to win."

A few hours later after successfully wiping the floor with Isaac and drawing almost the entire pub around the pool table after he proclaimed that drinks for everyone were on the winner, we take our leave. It takes us ages to escape the good natured ribbing he gets from the locals, many of whom ordered double and triple spirits when he got out his wallet.

"I guess that backfired. Having four brothers you'd figure I'd be better at pool."

We walk side-by-side in the same direction, having found out during our game of pool that Isaac's rented house is directly opposite mine.

"I did warn you I was playing to win," I tease good-naturedly.

I haven't had so much fun in ages, because despite his protests, he was playing to win, so the competition was friendly but fierce.

"That you did. I guess I'll learn to heed the warnings next time. I mean the fact that I didn't even pick up my cue during the first game should've clued me in to the fact that I was up against a fucking pool shark."

A hearty laugh falls from my mouth and echoes on the quiet, empty street.

"Sign of a misspent youth. Growing up where I did you could either hang around the park and do drugs and booze or hit up the Snooker club. I've always been into sport so the park and its illicit poisons never really enticed me. Plus, my brother liked to play, so we used any pocket money we had to pay for tables."

"Is he a pool shark like you?"

The question is innocent and a natural progression in our conversation, but it still jars me for a moment.

"He died when I was seventeen."

Talk about how to put a downer on a good night.

He's silent for a moment and I anticipate the usual response most people feel expected to give of 'I'm sorry', but instead he places his hand on my shoulder and quietly says, "That must have been hard for you."

I'm not sure which part sends a rush of warmth through me, the touch of his hand or the concern of his words.

"Yeah. I kinda lost my way for a while. When I say 'while' I should really say it's only recently that I've been getting my shit together."

"There isn't a time limit on grief." He talks like a man who knows.

"I guess not."

We walk a few minutes longer in silence and turn onto the entrance of our street. With each step, the air around us thickens. This is the part where we say goodbye and all of a sudden instead of feeling like this is the end of the night in the pub with a new friend, it feels like the end of a date. For a man who has only ever dated women, it's a confusing thing to feel those butterflies towards another man.

"This is me." Isaac stops walking outside a small, red gate and motions to a house similar in appearance to mine.

"And I'm just over there, so if you need to borrow a cup of sugar I suggest knocking the door of another neighbour because I don't buy any." I run my hand down over my broad chest and add jokingly, "My body is a temple."

I expect him to laugh but when our eyes clash after he follows the movement of my hand, all I see his heat, hunger and a need so brazen that when his lips part slightly and I see just the tip of his wet tongue, my cock stands up and takes notice so fast that I experience a head rush. All the blood in my body drains from my extremities and pools in my groin leaving me light headed.

He blinks just once, breaking our intense connection and I see the shutters come down and the lust get covered with a mask of friendliness.

"Well… Goodnight, Flynn. I had a great night with a new friend."

That word on his tongue sounds wrong.

*Friend.*

I'm going to blame lack of blood and oxygen to my brain for what I do next.

It takes just one step forward to put us toe to toe and the way his breath hitches in his throat tells me the move was both unexpected and welcomed. It's a complete turn on.

Wrapping my hand around the back of his neck, our

heights almost match meaning I only have to dip my head a fraction to bring my mouth to his but before I take his lips in a ferocious kiss I growl out, "Fuck friends."

# chapter 17

*Isaac*

The rasp of my stubble across his smooth skin sends shivers of want down my spine. When his tongue thrusts through my parted lips, he's not gentle or hesitant. He takes, he owns, and he pillages. Our mouths duel, chasing the need that pulses between us and I have never felt this level of desire for another person.

Which is why when I put both my hands on his firm chest and push him away, I curse myself for not just giving in and allowing him to take what he needs. What we *both* need.

"*Stop.* This-" I motion with my finger between us "-isn't going to happen. Not again." I pant out the words, my chest rising and falling frantically in an attempt to draw enough air into my lungs.

"I can't do this with you again. Once, fool on you. Twice,

fool on me, but three times makes us both as stupid as each other."

He drops his hands and rams them into his jean pockets, his shoulders slumping and his eyes unable to meet mine.

"I'm sorry, I thought… I shouldn't have…"

His embarrassment is palpable. The confused, hurt and ashamed expression on his face is almost my undoing. I don't want to shame him or hurt him, but I refuse to be used and then tossed aside again.

"Listen," I rest my hand on his shoulder, and he tentatively lifts his head to look at me. "I'm not going to lie and tell you that wasn't the best kiss I've had in a long time because it was." I smile softly and can't help but lick my lips to taste him once more. "But we've been down this road twice before, albeit in different circumstances. I haven't changed who I am, and I haven't stopped wanting you, but I'm not an experiment, Flynn and I'm not your punching bag for whatever issues you have…"

"I wasn't…"

I squeeze his shoulder and interrupt, "Please let me finish. I can see things are different for you and that you've changed but I'm still a man, Flynn, and you're still attracted to women only."

"I'm attracted to you. *Shit,* it's more than that, it's always been more than that." His eyes hold mine, and his face sheds his embarrassment to be replaced with a look of yearning. "I promise to try and explain and earn your forgiveness, and I do want to be your friend, but fuck if you don't make me a little crazy and I can't help but want to take this further." He closes the space between us once more and hesitantly lifts a shaky hand to my face, his palm caresses my jaw as his thumb skims my cheekbone. Unbidden, I lean into his touch, wanting more of this, needing more of him, consequences be damned.

"Can we at least try? Because this thing between us is only getting stronger. I know you feel it. Can we be friends who maybe…kiss? And stuff."

God, his shy goofiness, a direct contrast to the demanding kiss he just landed on me, begs me to take him in my arms and do more than just kiss and *stuff.*

Losing all of my common sense and falling deeper into his dark brown eyes and timid smile, I lean forward the few inches to whisper across his lips, "How about you come inside for a nightcap, and we can see if you still want to kiss… and stuff?"

His reply is to lean in further until our mouths seal in the softest of soft kisses. He exhales against my lips, his eyes remaining open and locked on mine when he says, "Invite me in, Isaac."

Then we are a blur of lips, tongue and wandering hands. I stumble backwards, dragging Flynn with me refusing to break our connection as I fumble through my pockets for the door key. Our mouths remain fused as I try and fail to get it into the lock and with a deep chuckle Flynn grabs the key from my hand, places one last kiss on my lips and effortlessly slides it into the lock, opening the door within seconds.

His cocky, confident smile surges straight to my cock when he says, "After you," and motions me in before him. The glimmer of the streetlight on his kiss-wet, swollen lips is almost enough to make me say 'fuck it' and continue this right here on my front doorstep. By the look on his face when he raises his eyebrow at me and smirks, I guess he can see my intention too easily. Where did the shy, geeky man disappear? Because the man leading me in through my front door is self-assured and assertive and it makes me want to force him down to his knees where I can wipe the smile off his face with my cock in his mouth.

Not a good image to have when you just more or less told him you'd go slow, Iz. Chill the fuck out, I mentally chastise myself as I walk through the house switching on lights and trying to ignore the warmth of the man only one step behind me.

"Did you want another beer? Or a hot drink?" I open the fridge and scan the contents while Flynn leans up against the counter behind me. I bet he's checking me out. I *hope* he's checking me out.

"I'll take a water, if you have one. I've got an early start in the morning. It wouldn't be good to show up on my second day with a raging hangover."

Ah, yes. The film. The entire reason we've been thrown together again hasn't entered my mind for the last few hours, but we both have important commitments tomorrow.

"True," I say as I swing around, pushing the fridge door shut with my foot, a bottle of water in each hand. "It's not

*Wicked Water,* but I'm hoping it'll do." I smile to show I'm joking, but nerves flit across Flynn's face before he does a good job of pushing them away and walks towards me. When I say walk, it's more like he stalks towards me, his sights firmly set on my lips and not the beverage I'm offering.

"Thanks." He takes a bottle from my hand and sets it down on the kitchen worktop, his eyes never leaving mine. "I'm not really thirsty for a drink."

One more step and his strong hands tug me forward so he can once more claim my mouth.

This kiss is unlike the last few. It's explorative, deep and slow. He uses his lips and tongue to memorise my mouth, his teeth nipping at the soft skin of my swollen lips before his tongue sweeps forward to soothe the sting. I can feel this kiss *everywhere.*

Not one to usually submit in these situations, I give as good as I get, mirroring his movements until the drinks are long forgotten, and our hands join in this sensual pursuit of getting to know each other better. In my quest to feel more of Flynn, and to touch more of his skin, I drop my full bottle of water on the floor and ignore the thud as it hits the tiles and rolls away across the kitchen.

My hands now free to explore, I use one to skim over the soft stubble on his head and the other to snake under his tight t-shirt until I feel the warm, firm skin of his lower back. With that initial touch, his entire body shivers and he drags me closer until we are chest to chest, thigh to thigh and groin to groin.

I can feel his thick erection as it rubs up against my rock hard cock and the groan that escapes my lips earns me a moan from Flynn followed by another shiver. Emboldened by his reaction, I test my luck further and rock up against him creating a delicious friction that will soon see me coming in my pants like a teenager dry humping his first date.

"*Fuuuck*. You feel too good," he pants against my neck after breaking our kiss to drag in some air. My hips continue thrusting, and he meets my fervour, rolling his cock against mine each time and increasing the intensity of the feelings flooding my body.

I lick along the pulse point on his neck before nibbling it with my teeth eliciting a hiss of pleasure to fall from Flynn's lips.

"Did I say..." he groans and sucks in a breath when I repeat the move, "kiss and stuff? I meant more. I need so much more, Iz."

This man is going to be my undoing because against my better judgment I want to give him more. I want to give him so much more that if I think about it for too long, it would likely scare both him and me.

Pulling back, I look into his heavy-lidded, lust-filled brown eyes and can't help but run my thumb over his plump lips. He reacts by taking the digit into his mouth and sucking it, *hard*.

"*Fuck*. I want to give you more. Let me make you feel good, baby."

*Baby?* Fucking baby? Where the hell did that ridiculous

pet name come from? In a blatant attempt to gloss over my slip of the tongue, pointless because Flynn's eyes widened at the endearment falling from my lips, I run my hand down to the front edge of his t-shirt and drag it out of his jeans. Slowly, I inch the fabric up over his body, first exposing his lickable six-pack, up over his firm biteable pecs and swiftly over his head until he's topless before me.

Flynn's body is a sight for sore eyes. It's a work of art, one I'd love to get in front of my lens again or even better, under my naked body.

Stilling my hands with his before they can reach the button of his jeans, he hesitantly licks his lips and says, "No. I want to make you feel good."

*Sweet baby Jesus.* Like I said, this man is going to be my undoing.

"You don't have…"

He silences me with a finger to my lips. "I want to, Iz. I need to. Let me taste you, let me make *you* come undone."

Before I can protest- not that I want to, I mean how often does a Greek God of a man beg you to let him taste you? Not often e-fucking-nough let me tell you -he slides his way down my body until he's kneeling on the hard ceramic floor at my feet.

The vision of the strong, powerful, sexy man on his knees for me and *only* me has my cock throbbing like a jackhammer. The thing is practically digging its way out of my pants.

With confident fingers, he makes quick work of the

buttons on my jeans and then he's sliding the denim off my hips and down my thighs, the backs of his hands skim across the hairs on my legs making my knees practically buckle. My boxers follow quickly until I'm standing above Flynn Phillips with the hardest cock I've ever had in my life.

He stares at it transfixed, his face reflecting a mixture of nerves, lust and a touch of apprehension.

I have to remember that although he's seen a cock before he's likely never seen another man's up close and personal and definitely not one that is seconds away from spurting all over his handsome face.

I close my eyes to push away the image of Flynn Phillips' gorgeous face painted in ribbons of my cum. *Fucking hell,* I'm about to make that vision a reality despite the fact he hasn't even touched my cock yet.

"*Fuck.* You're killing me here, babe." I can't help the groan of frustrated need that accompanies my words. I don't want to push him, but I'm kinda standing here with my raging boner pointing right at his lips while he wears a look that is part deer caught in the headlights and part starving diabetic with a sweet tooth locked in a chocolate factory.

"It's so fucking big." His words are both flattering and laughable. I mean every guy wants to be told he's massive but not when the person saying it looks a touch petrified. It's not as if my giant cock is going to kill him. Well, it might if he doesn't wrap his fat fucking lips around it in the next few seconds.

I huff out a small laugh and then fist my cock at the root,

angling the tip in his direction.

"It doesn't bite I promise, but it's not too late to back out," I whisper as I stroke up my length, then twist my hand over the head encouraging a bead of pre-cum to escape from the tip. I'm relieved to see him lick his lips at the sight and lean in a fraction closer, his eyes now showing more desire than nerves.

"I'm more afraid I might bite it, it's not like I'm a pro at this," he replies, his stare still fixed on the blush red head of my cock.

I tilt my hips forward a little until his lips are a hairsbreadth away and the heat of his mouth washes over my pulsing shaft. My body screams at me to take control and force my ridged length past his plump lips to sink into the wet heat of his hungry mouth. If he were anyone else, I would, but Flynn needs to take this final step. This is his choice to make and his last chance to back away.

My body feels coiled as tight as a spring, the pulse in my shaft an ache that borders on pain. Never have I wanted someone's mouth on me as much I do his.

*Suck my cock, Flynn. Take it.* I mentally beg.

Between one blink of my eyes and the next, I am engulfed in tight, warm, wet heat. There are no explorative licks, no hesitant whispers of lips. He takes my cock right to the back of his throat and instinctively swallows tearing a string of expletives from my mouth.

"*Fucking hell, Holy shit...*" My head tips back and I have to close my eyes and will my hips to remain still as he fucks me with his mouth, lavishing my cock with long licks and demanding control of my pleasure by hollowing his cheeks and sucking me with relentless enthusiasm. What he lacks in experience, he makes up for in eagerness. I'm seconds away from blowing my load right down the back of his throat and wouldn't that be embarrassing.

I look down into the lusty brown eyes that stare up at me through long, dark lashes. His lips reach the end of my cock, and he removes his mouth just enough to say, "I want all of you, Iz. Let go. I can take it."

His words, his mouth on my cock and his eyes filled with want for me and me alone, snap the cord on the last of my control.

I cup his jaw tightly with my left hand before slowly raising it and placing both hands on the back of his fuzzy head. With a movement born of the need for release, I plunge my shaft back into his open mouth, and he closes around the invasion, sucking, licking and humming his desire as my hips thrust and glide my length at an aggressive pace in a bid to chase my release.

He adds his hand into the mix, stroking his tight fist down to the base of my shaft in alternating movements to his naughty and talented mouth. The dual sensations plunge me over the edge.

"I'm going to come," I manage to warn him; giving him the chance to avoid a mouthful of everything I have to offer. Instead of pulling back, he increases his pace and slides his hands over my hips before digging his fingers into the cheeks of my arse. The move tears my orgasm from me and I come hard, rasping his name. My blunt fingernails dig into the soft scruff of his stubbled head, and he swallows everything I give him. Every. Last. Drop.

Ruined.

I'm totally fucking ruined.

# chapter 18

*Flynn*

Isaac Fox just came down my throat, and I fucking loved it.

His massive cock still pulses with aftershocks as I swallow down the last of his essence wishing I could do that again.

Watching him come undone because of *my* mouth has to be the single most erotic experience of my life.

And I want more.

More of him.

I want it all.

Every thought I had about being with him and what that made me has been obliterated with the throaty sound of my name on his lips and the salty flavour of his lust exploding across my taste buds.

As I kneel on the cold floor of his kitchen, his tall, leanly built frame towering over me, I don't feel cheap, submissive or used. I don't feel like any of the derogatory words I once used like *pussy boy, homo* or *fag.* I feel content, powerful and downright fucking horny for more.

My cock weeps with the need to come and play. It's practically crying in my pants, begging to be freed and to experience more of what Isaac Fox has to offer. Despite my burning need, I have no intention of allowing my cock anywhere near Isaac Fox.

Not tonight.

Tonight was about showing him I want him.

*Him.* No one else. I'm not afraid anymore. I'm not a coward about to spout hurtful words because I'm too chicken to face what's right in front of me.

I want a man. Not any man, this man.

Single, *straight,* Flynn Phillips aches with desire for another man.

After everything I went through when my brother took his life, after seeing the man who broke the last fragile thread Clark had that tethered him to this world, still living his life with his *wife* and *kids,* I had finally moved past the hate. Watching that man play happy families while my brother was nothing but ash on the wind, scattered on a beach and swallowed by the waves, had broken something inside me. It had festered and putrefied into something grotesque and ugly, but Isaac had changed all that.

No, I hadn't fully accepted why Clark left us or why he hid who he was from me, his brother and best friend, but I had finally accepted it was nothing to do with the talented and painfully attractive man standing above me.

"That was… wow. If I was marking you on your first attempt, that was a most definite eleven out of ten." Isaac's smile is teasing, his face one of a man still coming down after an intense orgasm. He looks a little giddy and a teeny bit shell-shocked. I like it a lot because I put that look on his too-handsome face.

Me, the straight boy with so much baggage I could fill a fucking airport carousel.

I rise to my feet, my ridged and over sensitised cock rubbing up against the back of my zip and causing me to wince and be forced to rearrange myself.

Isaac's gaze immediately focuses on the movement, and he takes a step forward. His semi-hard cock coming back to life with an impressive recovery time.

Warily, I take a step back, shoving my hands in my pockets to stop myself from reaching out to touch him, which is a bad idea because all it does is restrict the amount of space my raging boner has to breathe.

He stretches out his hands, hooking a finger from each into my belt hoops and playfully tugging me closer. His lips find mine in a whisper of a kiss, merely the fleeting touch of soft skin and he breathes, "Let me take care of you now."

*God, I want that.*

Pulling my hands from my pockets, I place both on the firm wall of his chest and push him away just at the moment he begins to dip down to his knees. I catch him off balance, and he stumbles, his eyes widening with shock and confusion before shuttering and becoming guarded.

This is the part he expected. He's been waiting for the penny to drop and for me to show my true colours. But, this time, he couldn't be more wrong.

He abruptly bends to grab the waist of his jeans and begins to drag them up the firm contours of his legs. His actions scream of a man ready to bolt, prepared for the worst.

I reach out and place my hands over his, stilling his movements, and he snaps his head up to stare at me.

"Say it. Do your worst. It's okay, Flynn. I'm a big boy. I can take it" His hands shake mine off, and he takes another step back before adding, "But once you're done, turn around and walk out of that door and never, *ever* take me for a fucking fool again." Anger pours off him in waves, and if I was about to say what he's preparing himself to hear, I think I'd be landed with a punch to the jaw at the very least.

That isn't my intention, though. Stopping him for reciprocating wasn't because I don't want him or because I'm ashamed of what just happened between us, it's because I want more than a quick blowjob on his kitchen floor.

With steady hands, I reach out once more and close the distance between our bodies. He remains stock still, waiting for me to prove him right.

"I know what you're thinking..." I begin, and he opens his mouth to interrupt but I'm not done, and so I silence him with a soft shake of my head. "You're waiting for the bile to flow from my lips, for the acid to pour from my lungs and for my disgust to burn everything in its path, including you."

When he doesn't deny it, I continue by making the same move he pulled on me moments ago. I hook my fingers into his jeans and tug him forward until we are practically chest to chest.

I can't help looking from his eyes down to his luscious mouth, wondering if refusing to have those juicy lips around my cock is the single most stupid thing I've ever done in my adult life.

"I don't want you to reciprocate and not because I feel I owe you one…" I lift my eyes to stare into his hazel ones. "But because I wanted, no I *needed* our first encounter this time around to be about you and not me." I shake my head and laugh lightly, "Not that I didn't enjoy what I just did, because I fucking did, so I'm not a complete saint." I release the grip of my right hand from his jeans and bring it up to cup his face, my skin tingling at the rough yet smooth sensation of his stubbled jaw across my palm.

"I've never had a relationship, Iz. I've fucked a lot of women, I've enjoyed their company, but it was never anything more than sex. My head is spinning and not just because you're a man but because I want more than that with you." I try and maintain eye contact, but my cowardice wins out. I drop my gaze back to his lips before finishing, "It's more than just sex with you, and I'm kinda putting myself out there and hoping you feel this thing between us just as deep, just as hard as I do. Because I'm going to look like a right tit if all you wanted was to get your rocks off with me."

# one

When I've finished admitting what I want, I lift my eyes to his hoping for acceptance and praying that he doesn't decide my fucked-upness isn't worth it. What I see in his hazel depths is indecision.

That's okay. I can work with that. I just tore off a layer of my soul and laid it at his feet, but he's more than justified to stomp all over it and use it as a rug or even a doormat. I deserve to have his mud-encrusted size tens trample all over me.

When he does speak, it hits me right in the solar plexus, knocking the air from my lungs and leaving me emotionally choked.

"I'm not a one-person kind of guy, Flynn. It's not me. I give, and I receive, and then I leave."

*Fuck. That hurts like a bitch.*

I don't realise I've closed my eyes until he whispers across my lips, "Open your eyes and look at me, Flynn fucking Phillips."

My lids snap open and I'm struck by the sheer emotion on his face when he says, "But this time I want to stay." He smiles sweetly before continuing, "Someone recently told me a change is as good as a rest. I want to see where this goes. I want to rest awhile with you."

Now, as I lay alone in my empty bed, I replay every second of the night. From the initial buzz that washed over me when he first entered the pub, to the way he bantered with everyone when I kicked his arse at pool.

I linger on the way my name poured from his lips as I drank him down, the silky smooth skin wrapped around his solid length and the taste of him exploding over my senses. But what I repeat more than anything is his parting words when he walked me to my door. Yes, he walked me across the street right up to my front door, his hand tightly holding mine the entire time.

"I meant what I said, Flynn. This is as new to me as it is for you, and I'd be a liar if I said I wasn't fucking petrified of the fallout, but as long as you're in this with me, I'm willing to take that chance. If you want me in your life, put me there. It's that simple."

He didn't wait for a reply. He placed a single, soft kiss on my lips that had my still steel hard cock begging for just one touch and then turned and walked back over the road to his place. He stopped when he got to his front door, turned and gave me a small salute.

*If you want me in your life, put me there.*

Can it be that simple?

Because I really fucking wanted him there.

# chapter 19

*Isaac*

I'd only seen Flynn in passing for the last couple of days. The next few weeks' filming were all going to be night shoots and between learning the ropes of my role as I go and watching playback of Flynn in his scenes- because if I couldn't see him in person I'd take his psychotic killer persona- neither of us had chance to say more than a brief hello to each other.

As I watched last night's recording and tried and failed to concentrate on the cinematics instead of obsessing over a sexy, bald and scarred Flynn, Jake walks into my small trailer as if someone has set his arse on fire.

"Rumour is you're fucking one of my actors."

"Straight to the point as always. Shouldn't you of all people be wary of listening to rumours? Wasn't there a media storm about a love-child you were supposed to have fathered in the not so distant past?"

I turn back around to the screen in front of me that I have unwittingly paused on a close-up image of Flynn.

"You're fucking Phillips? What the fuck, Iz!"

*Great. Just what I need.*

I spin back around in my chair and face my older brother. He glares at me, steam practically pouring out of his ears with the ferocity of his anger.

"*No.* I am not fucking Phillips." *Yet.* "And what fucking business is it of yours if I was? I've never got pissy with you about who you've stuck your dick into."

If possible, his fury intensifies, and I want to laugh at the comically ridiculous look on his face.

"It's my business because you are *both* working on my film. If things go tits up it's me that will deal with the repercussions. Besides the fact, he's a fucking straight man, Iz. For once can't you just stick to pussy and while you're at it, stick to pussy that has *nothing* whatsoever to do with my movie."

If there wasn't a shred of truth to his words, this would be the time that Jake and I would come to blows. It's never happened before, but then he's never got all up in my business before.

"I said," I grit through my teeth, my anger slowly rising to match his, "I'm not fucking Flynn Phillips. You can choose to believe me or not. We're friends. That's it."

The door to my trailer slams shut with a heavy bang but

not before I see the back of Flynn's shaved head as he leaves.

*Fuck. Fuck. Fuck me sideways.*

"Huh," Jake mocks. "From the way he just stormed out of here I'd say you're lying through your fucking teeth, brother."

"Fuck you, Jake," I say as I shoulder check him on the way out of the door, hot on Flynn's heels. Having him overhear the last tiny bit of our conversation isn't going to do me any favours and lying to my brother is a shit thing to do, but until I know what Flynn and I are to each other there is no way I'm spilling my guts and setting myself up to fall.

"Flynn! Wait up, slow down," I yell over the bustling noise of the cast and crew who are meandering through the various backstage areas.

"I know you can hear me, Phillips. Just wait a fucking minute would you."

I don't give a fuck about the amount of attention I'm drawing towards us. I'm not letting him walk away from this, from what we started the other night until he hears me out.

Flynn notices the stares and eyes that follow us as he power walks away from me and I chase after him like a lovesick girlfriend. So he picks up his pace, almost breaking into a full jog. He dodges past equipment and random set production and ducks down a tight passageway between two massive storage containers.

I make a lunge for him, my body colliding with his built frame, momentum carrying us both into the metal siding with a loud thump.

"I said to fucking wait a minute," I pant out between

harsh breaths while struggling to pin his front up against the container by using my entire body weight.

"Get the fuck off me!" He thrashes and jerks until I take a step back and he wheels on me, fists raised.

"You want to punch me? Take your shot. But I'm warning you. You'll only get one chance." I stare him down, waiting for the inevitable fist to my face. Instead, he stands there never lowering his arms, his body braced for violence, his chest heaving with the need to inflict pain.

"We're friends? That's it?" He finally drops his hands to spread them before him. "Are we friends with benefits? Bros with blowjobs?" He steps forward to pin me against the opposite container, and my back hits the metal with a dull thud.

"Or are we fuck all? Was this all a convenient way to pay me back for being a prick to you. Because I gotta say, Isaac, well fucking played. You win."

By now we are chest to chest but not in the good, 'I'm about to fuck you' kind of way, more like 'I'm about to rip your arms off and use them to beat you into a pulp' kind of way.

"You didn't hear the whole conversation. If you'll let me explain you'll realise what a complete idiot you're being right now."

*Wrong thing to say.*

"I'm being a fucking idiot? Me?" He growls out pushing into my chest like a silverback Gorilla before it tears it's opponent apart.

173

# one

There is very little height difference between us, maybe an inch, but where I'm leanly muscled, Flynn is built like a brick wall and the difference in our bodies has never been more evident than it is right now.

I shouldn't be so completely turned on by his aggression but fuck me I am. If he was to bring our lower halves closer with one small step forward he'd feel just how much.

Time to turn this testosterone show down a little.

"Yeah, you are." I temper my voice, removing any trace of anger and hoping to defuse his. "Jake accused me of fucking you and warned me away. The last thing I need is my brother on my case, and the last thing you need is your director on yours, so I told him what he needed to hear, nothing more nothing less." He's not buying this at all. So I continue, "Besides, it's the truth. We haven't *fucked* yet." I punctuate the f-word with a languid lick of my dry lips. A trick he doesn't miss and I'm close enough to see his pupils dilate and a flash of lust overtake the red mist in his stare.

I wait for his fist to make contact because taunting an angry bear is sure to get me mauled and it does, violently, But not by his hands, by his mouth.

With one brutal move, my arms are pinned to my sides, and his mouth is on mine. There is nothing sweet about this kiss, it's angry, it's violent, and it's sure to draw blood with our clash of teeth and duelling tongues. I refuse to submit, despite his strength immobilising me. He takes and I take back, he demands, and I force the kiss further until his hips thrust against mine, and our heavy cocks are angrily rubbed against each other. Much more of this and I'll be unable to walk or talk, but I don't care because this base need between us, this unmistakable raw hunger we have for each other is potent and all consuming. Two dominant males are fighting for control, neither willing to give in. But something is going to have to give.

I'm shocked when it's Flynn who capitulates. His thrusts turn from angry to sensual, his mouth breaking from mine enough for us both to take a long breath before he returns to lick over my bruised lips, lovingly soothing away the sting.

We slowly come down together until his forehead rests against mine and his hips lay flush against me.

"I want you so damn much it hurts." His honesty cuts me to the core, and I hate that I made him think I didn't want the same thing.

"Then take me," I offer, and I don't just mean in the biblical sense. As much as I want this man in my body, I want him everywhere else as well.

I'm rarely a bottom when I'm with men, but for Flynn, I'll be anything he needs.

A pained groan leaves his mouth, and he lifts his head to rest it against mine, cheek to cheek. His lips are perfectly placed to rasp into my ear, "Don't offer something you're not planning to give."

"What time do you finish tonight?"

He pulls his head back quickly, his eyes scanning my face searching for truth in what he thinks I'm about to say then admits, "I've finished for today. I'm not needed on set tonight."

I don't smile when I reply, I just stare into his dark brown eyes, needing him to see how much I'm offering him and how much I want him to take it. "Then take me home and fuck me, Flynn. I want your cock so deep inside me that I don't know where I end and you begin."

His entire body trembles at my words and I have to bite the inside of my cheek to stop myself from moaning out loud in reaction to his obvious need for me.

If I thought he'd ruined me before, I know without a doubt when he sinks inside me for the first time, he will fucking own me.

"Then what the hell are we still standing here for? I swear to God that if I don't get inside you soon I'm going to explode and I'd rather do that when I'm buried eight inches deep in you."

*Fucking ruined.*

# chapter 20

*Flynn*

I'm driving behind Isaac Fox, watching him ride that hot as fuck motorbike in head to toe leathers and all I can think is 'I'm about to fuck a man.' A man that turns me on and has made me harder than anyone else in my life.

I know the mechanics of what's about to happen, I've had anal sex with women before, albeit infrequently, but this is about more than me getting off, I want it to be good for him too. No, scratch that, I want it to be fucking amazing for him.

He doesn't come across as a man who gives up control in the bedroom easily, so the likelihood of Isaac being a regular bottom is low.

*Fuck.* Just thinking about anyone else sinking into my man has me clenching my fists on my steering wheel and has my blood pounding through my veins wanting to exact violence on anyone else to ever have touched him.

*My man.* I can't be sitting here thinking of him as my man. That's just absurd in every way.

*Then what is he?*

My friend? My lover?

I'm tossing around labels in my head when I see Isaac flick on his indicator and wave me towards an upcoming petrol station. I can't believe he needs to stop when I have a humongous boner rubbing up against the inside of my jeans just begging to be let loose.

I pull up behind him as he engages his kickstand and dismounts. The leather of those tight trousers ripples over his strong legs and pulls taut across his perfectly shaped backside. He's a fucking sight for sore eyes or a sore nob in my case.

Without removing his helmet, he flicks up his visor and lightly jogs towards me. I press the button to open my window and lean my head out as he approaches.

"I need to grab us some stuff. I, uh, don't have anything in the new place as I wasn't planning on… um, entertaining." His eyes blink quickly, and I swear if I could see his full face he'd be blushing. Before he has the chance to turn away, I reach out and snag his wrist, grabbing his attention. He looks at me in confusion, "You need something in there? I can grab it for you."

"No, and neither do you. I have everything we need at my place. I uh…" Now it's my turn to get a little embarrassed. "…stocked up on some stuff we might need the other day."

I know he's smiling because his eyes crinkle at the corners.

"You bought rubbers and lube?"

*Spell it out, why don't you.*

I quickly flit my eyes over the forecourt, a nervous gesture more than worry that he's been overheard.

"Yes," I hiss. "I got condoms and stuff."

"Lube. You can say it." His eyes crinkle further, and his shoulders shake silently. The fucker is laughing at me.

"I've bought fucking lube. Okay? Want me to announce it to half of Cardiff? Or are you going to get back on that sexy as fuck death trap you call a bike and get your fuckable arse back to my place before I give the old guy staring out of the window at us a full-on porn show and bend you over right here in this *Texaco* garage?"

At my mini rant, he full on belly laughs. The bastard.

"Easy, tiger," he chuckles. "I was just checking that we were on the same page. You keep saying 'stuff' and forgive me, but that could encompass just about anything."

"I meant fucking lube!" I yell a little louder than necessary, my voice echoing out over the thankfully empty forecourt.

He doesn't respond, and I watch as he leisurely strolls back to his bike, his shoulders shaking with mirth the entire way.

*Yeah, yeah. Laugh it up, buddy. I'll soon shut you up when I thrust my cock down your throat.*

He lifts his long leg over the body of his bike and mounts

the machine, straddling it with his legs. Isaac Fox all in leather on a motorcycle should be illegal.

With a wave of his hand, he pulls off, straight out of the garage and into the traffic with ease. I'm not so lucky and end up a couple of cars behind him, a lorry and an old Morris Minor blocking my view of his fine rear, making me even more tetchy.

Soon, but not soon enough, I'm pulling up outside my place and jumping eagerly from the car. Isaac is already stood outside my front door, leaning nonchalantly against the red tiled arch that frames the period style entrance.

Still clad in his bike leathers, he's enough to make anyone salivate. The man screams sex. And he's mine. All fucking mine.

Hello territorial, my name is Flynn. I should just piss in a circle around him and stake my claim.

"Took your time," he teases, unable to keep the dirty and delectable grin off his face.

I shrug, "Nothing to rush home for."

Before I can react, he pushes himself off the wall and cups my cock tightly with his large hand.

"Really? This doesn't feel like nothing," he smirks as his warmth permeates my jeans and engulfs my throbbing shaft.

"Get. Inside. Now." I grit out between my teeth fighting a battle against my raging libido. "Enough teasing. It's time for me to take what you promised."

Isaac's eyes flare at my words, and after one last tight squeeze of my cock that almost makes my knees buckle, he steps back and motions to the door.

"Then invite me in, babe. I never go back on a promise."

The cocky way his eyebrow arches and his full lips tips up on one side has me all but storming past him with a desperate need to open the fucking door and get him in my bed before I do something stupid like strip him naked on my doorstep.

The click of my key opening the lock echoes through the heavy silence. A noise that signifies this is real, this is happening, this is me inviting Isaac Fox into my bed.

Lust burns thickly through my veins and my fingers shake with apprehension, nerves bubbling up through my gut making the few steps I take into my house seem abstract and surreal. It's like I'm walking through a filtered world where everything else is blurry, except him. When I turn to face him at the bottom of my stairs, his masculine beauty dazzles me in sharp focus, stripping away the haze clogging my thoughts and bringing me right back to the here and now. Right back to him.

I shake off my anxiety and extend my hand, palm up, for him to take. He doesn't hesitate, not even for a second, and soon his warm skin engulfs mine, and I turn to lead him up the stairs.

From the moment we touch, everything else disappears. Our hands stay linked until I push open the door to my bedroom, and I watch as he takes in the only thing in the high-ceilinged room. A king size bed covered in white sheets. There is nothing about this room that screams home, no knickknacks, no pictures, not even a wardrobe with clothes. All my stuff is stored in one of the spare bedrooms. I only use this room to sleep. And now to fuck.

"I like what you've done with the place. It looks just like mine." He chuckles and shakes his head, and I can picture a similar set up across the road. One I'll hopefully get to see in the near future, or we can just come here. I plan on *coming* here *a lot.*

"Enough chit-chat. You promised me something, and I'm ready to collect." I spin around to face him, my hands making quick work of the button fly of his leathers.

"Whoa, slow down," he stills my movements with his hands. "This isn't a race. I'm not leaving anytime soon, how about we take our time." He snakes his hand around the back of my neck and tugs my lips to his. "I plan on savouring every second, Flynn Phillips. I've wanted this, wanted *you* for so fucking long. I need to remember everything about the first time we're together. Every kiss," he places a soft one on my mouth "Every lick," he runs his tongue over my top lip, eliciting a full body shiver. "Every touch," he skims his hands down the sides of my neck, over my chest and around my waist where he uses them to squeeze my arse cheeks. "Every moan," he thrusts his tongue into my mouth earning him that very sound from the back of my throat. "Every thrust," he punctuates his words with a delectable roll of his hips bringing our cocks together with a delicious friction.

Panting in my ear, he places wet, open mouthed kisses down my neck until he reaches my collar bone, "I want to remember every fucking second."

Then we are a tangle of hands and tongues. Of drugging kisses and eager bodies.

His jacket and shirt end up the floor to be quickly joined by mine. My fingers continue their quest to unbutton his leather trousers, while his push my jeans down over my hips allowing my aching cock to spring free. Yeah, commando. Nobody can say I wasn't ready for this, ready for him.

"I needed you naked hours ago," I rasp across the sensitive skin that surrounds his nipple.

"And now you have me." He steps out of his leathers and boxer briefs, his heavy cock bouncing with his movements to slap against his lower stomach. With strong arms banded around me, he drags me backwards to the bed where I land on top of him, and his legs fall open to cradle me.

The position allows our bare, straining shafts to finally rub up against each other skin to skin, and we gasp into each other's mouths at the contact.

Wrapping a large hand around both our lengths, he squeezes before tugging our cocks with smooth strokes. Their sensitive heads rub together when we thrust in sync with his movements. Pre-cum dribbles from both tips, creating natural moisture that slicks our rigid cocks with the evidence of our need, creating the perfect lube. It's too much, a few more thrusts and it will all be over, and I don't want to come until I'm buried deep inside Isaac.

"*Stop*, I, ungh, I need to be inside you, and this feels too fucking good," I groan into his firm chest.

## one

He gives a husky chuckle and lifts my head with his free hand to bite my bottom lip, quickly soothing the sting with a soft swipe of his tongue. With one last firm stroke, he twists the palm of his hand as he reaches our weeping tips and rubs yet more of our desire over our sensitive flesh.

"I knew it would be like this. I knew I'd never get enough." His heavy-lidded eyes search mine needing to see the desire he's feeling reflected back.

I reply with my lips on his, showing him with my mouth instead of words that I feel it too.

My fingers trail down over his chest, lightly pinching the tight bud of his nipple as I explore his body. Smooth skin gives way to a trail of soft hair leading me in the direction of his straining cock. I break our kiss to follow the path of my fingers with my tongue, and as his body trembles with desire, I nuzzle my nose into the trimmed hair at his groin, inhaling his earthy, clean scent.

The difference between loving a man with my mouth over a woman isn't lost on me, as I soak in every masculine inch of him. From his firm muscles and hard ridges to his salty taste when I flick the tip of my wet tongue over the pearly bead of pre-cum that decorates the swollen head of his cock. His hips thrust upwards and his back arches, seeking out more. More touch, more sensation, more of me. I give him what he needs when I slowly lick him from root to tip before swallowing him down as far as I can go gaining me a delicious agonised moan.

One of my hands encircles his base, while the other

skims over his taint, stroking, teasing just enough to add another layer to the sensations blanketing his body. I want him on the brink. I want him begging me to fuck him.

I feel his body shift as he props himself up on his elbows to watch me. When our eyes clash, a groan escapes my throat, and he shivers at the vibration on his sensitive, engorged flesh.

"Where's the lube? Use your fingers on me, Flynn," he all but begs, his hips rising and falling with my ministrations.

After one last, long lick, I rise and drag my body over his making sure every part of me touches him, stimulating us both with the erotic sensation of hot skin touching hot skin.

When we are face to face, I waste no time in claiming his mouth, transferring the taste of him on my tongue, eliciting yet another deep moan from us both.

"It's in the bathroom, I'll go and get it, but I want you waiting for me. By the time I get back I want you on your hands and knees, and I want that firm arse in the air, begging for my touch."

I tug at his lower lip with my teeth as I painfully drag myself away from his heat. If I don't get up now, I never will.

*Why didn't I have the lube and condoms in my bedroom? Idiot.*

Iz flops back on the bed, raising himself on one arm to watch me walk away. I try not to rush, hoping to remain calm enough that when I get back to the naked man in my bed, I'll have enough self-control to prepare him for me, to make this good for him and not plunge my cock straight into his tight heat without thought for his comfort.

*I'm minutes away from fucking Isaac Fox.*

I grab the condoms and lube from the bathroom cabinet and catch a glimpse of myself in the mirrored door. My lips are wet and swollen, my jaw red with stubble rash and as I lean closer I see slight indentations to the skin on my neck, right at the place it meets my shoulder.

Teeth marks. That randy fucker has left his mark. That's going to raise a few eyebrows in make-up tomorrow.

I trail my fingers across his mark and catch myself smiling. The Flynn looking out at me from the mirror looks good. He looks happy, and he looks like a man about to get everything he never knew he wanted.

"Hurry the fuck up, would you or else I'm gonna finish myself off," Isaac shouts from the bedroom.

"Don't you fucking dare. Don't even touch yourself, that cock is mine," I holler back.

The man in the mirror smirks at me. It's a cocky grin, one that says 'You lucky bastard.' *Don't I fucking know it.*

When I walk back into the bedroom, Isaac is positioned exactly how I instructed on all fours with his perfect arse in the air. His head, which hangs down between his shoulders with his forehead resting on the bed, lifts and he looks at me over his shoulder.

"You're killing me here, babe."

My cock twitches at the affectionate term combined with the sensual look in his eyes.

Instead of replying, I stride towards him with purpose. I

drop the condoms on the bed and flick open the cap on the lube, pouring a generous amount into my hand and allowing the cool liquid to warm slightly against my skin. Kneeling on the bed behind him, I use my free hand to skim over his back from neck to tailbone, and he practically purrs, arching into the contact like a man starved of touch.

My lubed hand dips underneath to wrap around his rock hard shaft, while the hand skimming his back continues down to the smooth globes of his biteable backside. With deliberate movements, I run a single finger down his crack until I feel the puckered skin of his hole. It twitches under my gentle touch, and his hips thrust forward into my waiting hand.

"Need, more," he pants. "Quit fucking teasing me and fuck me with your fingers."

"Bossy much." I swot at his arse cheek with an open hand creating a spine-tingling smack and Isaac's head snaps back on a roar of frustrated desire.

"Stick. Your. Fucking. Fingers. In. Me. *Now.*"

"Say please." I mock, once again circling his tight hole with just the tip of one finger.

"*Fuck You.*"

"Nah, I think I'd rather fuck you."

Releasing his cock, I part his cheeks with one hand and bring my slick fingers to his clenched opening.

The time for teasing is over. Using one finger to start, I push the pad of the slippery digit against his pucker and massage the tight ring of muscle until Isaac is thrusting into thin air. When he's oblivious to anything else except the delicious pressure on his forbidden hole, I push past the initial resistance until his hot body swallows my pointer finger up to the second knuckle.

"*Fuck,* more. Give me more."

"Patience. I don't want to hurt you. Let me make this good."

"You're not going to hurt me. I need fucking more." He's panting and writhing, and I want to stop exploring with my fingers and dive in deep with my cock.

Working that digit in and out, over and over again, I grab the lube and pour some directly on his opening until it dribbles onto the sheets below. When I have him thoroughly drenched I ease in a second finger and plunge both to the hilt, nailing his prostate and extracting a garbled groan of random curse words to fly from Isaac's lips.

"*Ah-motherfucking-yes-right-there*"

Repeating the move, I work his hole and scissor my fingers to open him up for my cock. My fit-to-burst cock.

When he's writhing beneath me, his hips seeking friction for his heavy, aching shaft, I remove my fingers, earning me a whimper from Isaac. Rubbing the excess lube from my hands on the sheets and with impressively fast movements, I sheath myself with a rubber.

My legs bracket his spread thighs, my hand finds his shoulder, and achingly slowly I place the tip of my covered cock at his entrance.

"Do it, fuck me, babe. I need it," he encourages, pushing

his arse back until his eager hole swallows the very tip of my cock.

Moving both hands to his hips which I swear I'm going to bruise with my tight grasp, I still his movements and slowly, so fucking slowly, edge myself into his body.

He's so fucking tight and unbelievably hot. It takes all my willpower not to just fuck him hard and fast when his willing body squeezes the last of my control. Inch by fucking painfully incredible inch I push myself deeper until I'm buried to the hilt inside Isaac Fox. When I bottom out, and my balls rest against his smooth skin, he releases a gloriously sinful moan, and his inner muscles tighten even further. Without withdrawing, I grind myself against him and slide my hand around his waist to grip his bobbing shaft.

"Flynn, you have to… I need to… you've got to," he pants incoherently. But I know exactly what he wants because it's the same thing I do, he wants me to move.

I lean over his back until I'm fully covering him, one hand on the bed to steady myself, the other gripping his cock like a vice and as I pull back my hips to slide slowly out of him, I place my lips on the curve of his neck where it meets his shoulder.

When only my tip remains inside his hot channel, I angle my hips and thrust forward at the same time as I open my mouth and bite down into his skin.

"*Yeeeeesssss,*" he all but screams when I repeat the move and nail that spot deep inside him that makes him see stars.

"You're. Mine. Now," I growl out single words with each

thrust.

"You've put your mark on me, and I've claimed you."

I get in three more thrusts punctuated with, "Don't. You. Forget" before he's roaring out his orgasm, his seed painting my sheets and spilling over my hand at the same time as mine barrels through me catching me completely off guard and stripping the air from my lungs. His arms shake, the power of his orgasm stripping him of strength as the aftershocks of mine ripple through my body. We collapse in a sweaty heap. My weight forcing him deep into the mattress, likely restricting the air into his lungs but he's not complaining so I'm not moving.

I'm lying, balls deep inside another man, with my chest plastered to his back and the remnants of his release clinging to my fingers and I've never felt more at peace.

Why did I ever fight this?

Why did I ever think I could win against the power this man has over me?

He owns me.

# chapter 21

*Isaac*

"Can't breathe," I cough reluctantly.

Flynn's substantial weight has me pinned to his mattress as he sprawls across my back after having just fucked me into next week and collapsed on top of me.

If I could get more air into my lungs, I'd let him stay right where he is because his weight feels good. Right.

"Pretend you're underwater. Just give me five more minutes," he grumbles into my ear making no attempt to get off me.

I use the last of the air in my lungs to huff out a laugh before I buck my hips in a useless attempt at dislodging his weight.

We both groan as his cock slips free.

"What did you do that for? I was comfortable," he

grumbles like a big kid before rolling off me onto his back and allowing sweet blessed air into my lungs.

I roll onto my side to face him and hook my leg over his, dragging his limp body across the smooth sheets until he's pressed up against me.

"Yeah, were you? Well, I wasn't, and I'm sure you wouldn't want to be responsible for my early demise."

I lean my head on his broad and sweat-damp chest, inhaling deeply and letting his scent wash over me like a soothing balm.

"Did you just sniff me?" he asks, wrapping his arm around my shoulders and absently playing with the ends of my hair.

"What if I did?" I throw back, revelling in his relaxed and comforting touch.

He only sighs in response, his arm tightening around me until our bodies are flush.

"That was fucking unbelievable," he mumbles into my shoulder, a languorous roll of his hips has his rubber clad, semi-hard cock pushing into my thigh, leaving a sticky trail in its wake.

"Shouldn't we go and clean up?" I ask, unbothered but looking for a reaction.

"Nope." He thrusts again. "I'm good right here."

We lie in each other's arms, a comfortable silence surrounding us. It's the kind that soothes, the kind that tells you you're with someone special, the kind that binds you to another person because it doesn't create distance, it closes it.

I'm halfway between sleep and awake when his voice rumbles over my skin. "Tell me something, something good."

"Like a fairy tale? You want a bedtime story to send you off to sleep?"

He pinches my side hard, and I yelp.

"No, you funny fucker, something good that's real. I've been living a good life, but it hasn't felt real for a long time. Tell me something about your life that's good."

"That's easy," I reply while trailing my fingertips up and down his arm. "Ivy-Leaves and Arty."

He rises enough to look into my face, "Cartoon characters?"

I chuckle at his scrunched up face, "My brother Josh's kids. I stayed with them for the last year, and they kind of took over my life."

"He gave his kids weird names. How come you took a year off to stay with them?"

I lift my hand and trace my fingers over the thick arch of each of his brows, his eyes closed at my touch, his mouth parting slightly on a heavy exhale.

"Josh lost his wife. She died suddenly after childbirth. He lost the love of his life, his soulmate and best friend. Added to his grief was a new born baby and toddler to care for, and for a long time he struggled. They needed me."

His eyes flick open, and I drop my hand to my side. He looks at me intently. His gaze was searching the depths of mine seemingly stunned by my admission.

"You sacrificed your career and put your life on hold for

193

them." It's a softly spoken statement, not a question.

"It wasn't a sacrifice."

"Yes, it was." He leans in and kisses me softly, sweetly and with meaning. When our lips part, he rests his head back on his hand and just looks at me.

The moment feels heavy, weighted down with emotions too strong to be felt this soon. Needing to remove his intense appreciation of me, I ask a question of my own. One that's been on the tip of my tongue since the night at the pub.

"How old was your brother when he died?"

His body tenses and the look of adoration on his face that was making me uncomfortable morphs into one of discomfort. I immediately regret asking, and I'm about to tell him not to answer when he quietly speaks.

"Nineteen. He was two years older than me to the day. We shared everything, including our birthdays."

I shuffle my body further down the bed and place my head on his chest, giving him the opportunity to speak without me staring and making it more difficult.

"Clark and I were like chalk and cheese, but we fit, you know." He begins to run his fingers through my hair. "He was slight with curly auburn hair that he absolutely hated. Where I was sporty and popular in school, he was reserved and shy, but he had the most sarcastic sense of humour that often got him into trouble at home." He chuckles lightly, lost in a memory and my head jiggles around on his chest with the vibrations of his controlled laughter.

"What happened? Was he ill for very long?"

His body stills completely, and his hand stops dead in a tangle of my hair.

"You don't have to keep talking about him if you don't want to."

He takes a deep, shaky breath and his hand resumes its movement, sifting his fingers through the longer strands at the top of my head.

"He hung himself from a tree in the yard of the construction company where he was a carpenter's apprentice."

*Shit. Shit. Shit.* What do you say to someone who has experienced that level of loss?

Nothing. There are no words to offer, so I pull him a little closer and squeeze him a little tighter. Telling him with my actions that I'm here, with him.

*I'm here for you.*

"Clark could make anything with his hands. Give him materials, and he would create masterpieces, give him scraps of wood, and he would make items of use and beauty." He lifts his head from his hand and lays down flat on the bed, pulling me with him. If he wants to talk for hours, I'm not going to stop him. The way he speaks, it's as if he's never told anyone any of this before.

"The month before he died, he finished this amazing table for my mother's birthday. His boss had given him some wood, to me it looked like half a rotten tree trunk, but he made this unbelievably incredible coffee table. He sliced down the trunk lengthways, so the top of the table had all the tree rings exposed. Years and years of this tree's life revealed like infinite perfect circles of existence."

His voice tremors when he continues.

"Just a few weeks later the hands that created the table that still sits proudly in my parents' living room were cold and limp. The life he showcased in that old tree stump, no longer flowing through his veins." The next words are wrenched from his throat as if they cause him physical pain.

"He went to the yard on the weekend when the place was closed. It's set back off the road and down a narrow lane so he knew nobody would find him until Monday." His body trembles and I want to beg him to stop because I can feel his hurt, the pain of this retelling a brutal open wound that I can tell has not scabbed over despite the passing of years.

"He climbed the tree that sits towards the back of the property with a bottle of vodka and a bag full of pills. There he penned a note addressed to our mother. The letter begins by saying he's not doing this to hurt anyone, and the more he drank and with each handful of pills he swallowed, his words start to jumble, his reasons and thoughts mutating into a nonsensical string of nothingness."

I can feel his shivers increase into full body shakes and I lift my head needing to be closer to him, needing to take away this burden. What I see when I look into his face guts me. His eyes are squeezed shut and rivers of tears coat his cheeks.

"Babe, don't keep talking if it's too hard for you. I didn't know, and I would never have asked the question and made you relive all this had I known." I kiss his forehead and clutch him to me, trying to tell him he's not alone. I've got him.

With a ragged inhale he shakes his head and continues, "He dosed himself with a lethal amount of booze and pills to be able to go through with it. He fell unconscious with the rope around his neck." Sobs choke his last few words.

"He couldn't do it. He couldn't... so he sat there, up in that godforsaken tree just waiting to pass out and let gravity steal his last breath. He died alone, Iz. And nobody found him for over twenty-four hours."

"I'm so sorry, babe. I'm so fucking sorry." I absorb his pain, kissing his scrunched up forehead over and over again, gently rocking this strong, powerful man in my arms until his sobs ease and completely spent, he falls asleep in my arms.

*Love hurts. It gives, and it takes away. It's brutal with its beauty.*

Holding Flynn Phillips tightly to my body I understand I'm putting myself at risk. I'm gambling with love, toying with the inevitability of pain because if I allow this man to burrow any further into my soul, I'll be giving him the power to annihilate me.

*Is love worth it?*

Josh and Flynn's stories tell me it's not. They tell me that I need to guard myself and remove that risk. This thing between Flynn and me can't go any further than this.

With a heavy heart and acute pain in my chest, I careful release Flynn and cover him with his white linen sheets. Then I slide out of his bed but not before placing one last kiss on his soft lips.

He exhales heavily at the contact, but he doesn't wake. So I grab my discarded clothes and quietly leave the room.

*It's the best for both of us.*

Neither of us is emotionally ready for anything more than sex. Tomorrow I'll tell him before it's too late. Before either of us puts our hearts on the line.

# chapter 22

*Flynn*

I haven't seen Isaac for four days.

The first time I have sex with a man and I decide in our post-coital glow to spill my guts and lay out most of my skeletons.

Awesome idea Phillips, way to fucking go.

I've never told anyone about how Clark committed suicide. I even skipped most of the details during therapy, finding it too hard to describe the last moments of my brother's life.

I didn't get to tell Isaac the reason why Clark thought his pain was too great to overcome, or should I say the catalyst that pushed him over the edge, because even I know that I can't blame just one person for my brother's issues. It was a combination of factors, ones he kept well-hidden even from me.

I had crumbled into a pathetic mess before I got that far and after sobbing myself to sleep in his arms, I woke up alone.

Disorientated and aching all over, I dragged myself out of bed. The used condom still on my now soft cock was a visual reminder of what had happened between us. I thought Iz would be downstairs or at the very least, in the shower.

But he was gone.

My house was empty, and the sun had long ago set.

I toyed with the idea of going over to his house and talked myself out of it. Maybe he had somewhere he needed to go and didn't want to wake me before he left? Maybe he had a family emergency?

Four days later and those maybes have died a sad and pitiful death. He's avoiding me.

When I ask around, trying and failing to not look overly interested in where the film's cinematographer has disappeared, I find out he's at another set location despite his schedule having him down as being here in Cardiff with me.

"You're up in ten minutes. All principles on set."

I nod in acknowledgement towards Callie, the young production assistant who has just given me my ten-minute warning and continue to stare directly ahead. My scarred face mocks me from the mirror. The realistic prosthetics a visual reminder of the internal lesions I carry. With a deep breath, I stare into my face and decide that it's long past the time to be rid of my festering wounds.

With determination I haven't shown for quite a while, I stare at my reflection and promise, "I'm coming for you, Isaac Fox. You can run, but you can't hide." Grim, my alter ego in the mirror agrees.

Today's scenes require nothing more from me than hanging around in the background. I have no lines to deliver and no direct screen time for the next couple of days. That's fine with me. I'm not sure I could concentrate on delivering a performance with any real believability anyway. My head is all jumbled up, and only one man can make that right.

Jake, Isaac's brother and my director, has also been avoiding me where possible. Yes, he gives me direction on set and is polite to me backstage, but we used to share a joke or have conversations about fitness. Now, he's distant, and I dare say aloof towards me.

I guess if he thinks I'm using his brother then his attitude towards me makes sense. God forbid if he found out exactly how I treated his brother previously, I think he'd lay me out on my arse, after firing me of course. But things are different, at least I thought they were.

"Okay, folks. That's a wrap for today. See you bright and early at five tomorrow morning." Jake dismisses us and leaves the set to go into the editing room and run through today's footage.

What I'm about to do may be foolish, but I'm at the point

where I couldn't give a fuck. I wait until the set clears and walk right up to the trailer that contains the editing suite, rapping my knuckles on the door sharply. I don't pause to be invited in I just push it open and step inside. Luckily, Jake is alone. He's likely dismissed the techs to review the scenes on his own before calling them back in to clean them up. He swivels in his chair to face me, a pleasant, professional smile on his face.

"What can I do for you, Flynn?"

Looking him straight in the eye, I realise I'm going to appear quite confrontational, but I'm struggling to keep my emotions in check.

"I've been looking for Isaac for a few days, and I wanted you to get him to call me."

"I didn't realise you two knew each other that well, is there something I can help you with?" His tone holds a bite of sarcasm.

"No, only Isaac can help me. So if I could get his number from you, or if you could pass on mine, I'd appreciate it."

He spins back around in a move to dismiss me and throws over his shoulder, "I don't think that's a good idea."

*Yeah, I'm about to get fired.*

"With all due respect, I didn't ask for your thoughts. I asked you for his number." I try and fail to keep the ire from my voice, and it gets the reaction I expected.

He flings himself back around to face me and stands, the momentum leaving his empty chair spinning like a top.

"With all due respect, Mr Phillips, I own you for the next

few weeks, so *everything* is my fucking business." His eyes blaze with fury, and he steps right up into my personal space in a move made to intimidate. "Whatever the fuck is going on between you two is jeopardising my movie, so the answer is no. I will not play go-between, and I will not be giving you his number."

I bite down so hard I'm surprised my teeth don't snap but I manage not to clench my fists and knock my boss on his arse.

With a herculean effort I grit out, "If you have any issues with my work, then and only then will I allow you to talk to me like you own me. *Nobody* fucking owns me, but one person has come close. So you can imagine how fucking determined I am to fix whatever the hell has gone wrong between us." I step forward enough to show that I will not be backing down. "What I do and what your brother does in our free time has nothing to do with you. Trust me when I say, the only person that can make me stay away from Isaac is him."

He matches my stance, his shoulders widening, his aggression palpable. "The fact he's avoiding you says it all, don't you think? If my brother wants a re-run fuck, he'll come and find you, I'm sure. Now if we're done here, I'll see you on set in the morning. I have work to do, and I want to get home to my wife and kid and not be caught up here firing one of my actors for his disrespect."

I've reached the end of my tether. He can fucking fire me. I'm past caring.

# one

"Fuck you very much, Mr Fox. You know where I am if you want to make good on your threats."

With those as my parting words, I turn and leave the trailer. As soon as I'm out of earshot, I spin and punch my fist straight through a giant set piece. Yeah, if I wasn't fired before, I likely am now.

The act of violence does nothing to quell the anger bubbling through my veins like acid, and I pull back my fist to do some more damage. Before I take the swing, a hand lands on my shoulder and I spin around faster than a bullet ready and willing to let my fury out on a person instead of a fake stud wall.

My fist falls redundantly at my side when I see before me the last person I ever expected, but the only person I've ever wanted. Stood behind me hands raised his palms facing outwards in the universal sign for 'don't attack', is the man that's been avoiding me for four long days.

I blink, expecting to see someone else when I open my eyes, believing that I must have conjured up his handsome face and intense hazel stare.

I want to be angry with him, I really do. I want to re-ball my fist and unleash all the pain of abandonment he's made me feel these last few days. But I can't because all I feel is relief.

"You've been avoiding me."

"I have," he nods honestly.

"Why?" I have to ask. The whys are always the things I struggle to understand.

He turns and looks over his shoulder, checking to see if anyone is watching us before turning back to look at me and answering, "Because I'm a coward."

*That's it? He's a coward. Yeah, well, you and me both.*

"And now? Is this you being brave?"

"No," he reaches forward to take my hand and whispers, "this is me being selfish. Take a walk with me?"

We leave the set separately with plans to meet at the same park where we initially bumped into each other. I drive home after having my fake scars and makeup removed with my gut a ball full of worry. This feels like the end when it never really began.

Instead of heading straight to our meeting place, I drive home and park my car on the street, choosing to walk the couple of minutes to the park and attempt to clear the tangle of thoughts in my head.

By the time I walk through the wide open gates and step onto the path that will lead me directly to Isaac, I have a plan. It's not a great one, but it's all I have. The plan is to simply not allow Isaac to walk away from this, from me.

I spot him before he sees me. He's sitting alone on a bench that overlooks the River Taff, his stare fixed on the fast flowing water, his hands braced underneath each leg. Even from this distance, I am drawn to him. Not just to the way he looks or the way he makes me feel, I am attracted to every part of him.

# one

With him, I've laughed, and I've cried. I've experienced all-consuming need and mind-blowing pleasure. I've shared my scarred soul and broken apart in his arms. But more than all that, I've lived. With him, I live.

I approach him slowly, only a slight twitch of his shoulder telling me he feels my presence. When I sit silently next to him, only a few inches away, the distance between us seems like miles.

"You came."

"You asked."

Birds flit above our heads from tree to tree, people jog, walk and ride past us, while fluffy clouds skim the blue sky painting a picture perfect scene. I appreciate none of it. My senses attuned to the man beside me, anticipating and expecting his rejection.

*It's only what I deserve.*

"I'm sorry I left the other night."

"Why did you? I mean, I think I know why but I'd rather hear you say it." I twist the leather cords on my wrist, rubbing my thumb over the little silver anchor plaited into the centre. The ends are worn and frayed, and it's doubtful it will stay on my wrist much longer, but until it breaks and falls off it's my only memento of my brother. I bought it for his eighteenth birthday. The anchor was to symbolise his wanderlust. Clark always said he was going to travel the world one day. Wearing this part of him kept him close and as my career took me from country to country it gave me a way to fulfil his dream.

Isaac sighs heavily, and I tilt my face to carefully watch

him as he battles with his explanation.

"When you told me about your brother…"

"I shouldn't have. It was the wrong thing to share after we'd just fucked." My tone is derisive, and I regret the words as soon as they leave my mouth.

He finally turns to face me. "We did more than just *fuck*, Flynn. Don't deny it just because I've hurt you and you want to inflict a few wounds on me of your own."

He returns his gaze to the water and continues, "When you shared Clark's story, I felt it. Every word and syllable hurt. I wanted to absorb your pain and take it away for good." He drops his head and looks at his hands. "I've seen that level of damage before. I've lived it vicariously through my brother Josh. I've seen his despair. I've felt the ripples of its repercussions. Grief is the price we pay for love."

We are both silent while I absorb his words. He's not making any fucking sense. His answer is ridiculous for more reasons than avoiding the possibility of falling in love with me.

"So you'd rather push me away than ever love me? Is the possibility of loving me not enough to make it worth the risk? Because I thought we were going to see where this goes, Iz. We're at the beginning of something, something worth the risk. Besides, you have others you love. Your parents, your brothers, Ivy-Leaves and Arty. Would you walk away from them to ensure you never got hurt?"

"No."

"But you're walking away from me, someone who hasn't

even gained your love yet? I have to say that's the biggest load of bollocks I've heard in a long time. Why don't you just say it? Thanks for the fuck, Flynn but I got what I wanted, and the payback tasted as sweet as I thought it would."

That gets a reaction from him other than the reserved indifference that's been wafting from his skin like a bad smell.

"Do you think I let you fuck me as revenge? Surely I would have fucked you for that theory to work?" he sneers as he leans across the bench bringing us almost nose to nose.

"I told you I haven't done this before and less than an hour ago I told you I walked away because I was a coward. I'm scared I'm going to hurt you, Flynn. Can't you see that? Yes, I walked away to save my skin, but I also left to save yours. What if I fuck up? You've had enough people leave you, and I didn't want to add to the list."

"So you left anyway?"

"Yes, I left anyway, before this thing between us grew and planted roots."

"And now?" I don't care how pathetic it makes me look. I'll beg if he wants.

His eyes sparkle with what looks like hope, and a shiver runs through me. Has he changed his mind?

"Now, I know I was wrong. So fucking wrong, Flynn. But I'm not sure if this was the fuck up to end all fuck ups. I don't know if you'll give me another chance."

"I seem to recall you gave me more than one second chance."

That sparkle in his eyes flickers into a full blown light

208

show, and he leans in even closer. To everyone around us we look like two lovers about to kiss. In my past even thinking about touching another man inappropriately in public would have sent me over the edge, would have sent the old Flynn over the edge. The new Flynn wants it more than his next breath, and I couldn't give a fuck if we're recognised and if it's splashed across the front page of the morning papers.

"And am I worthy of the same?"

"Yes." I haven't even fully finished the word before his mouth is on mine. It's a kiss that says sorry, one that talks of new beginnings and smothers all regret.

"Come home with me, babe. Let me show you how sorry I am for not staying, for hurting you and for making you think, even for one second that you are not worth the risk."

*Babe.* I'm turning into a right wuss because that word on his lips sends tingles down my spine every time.

"*Fuck.* I can't. Elaina, my personal assistant, is meeting me at my place in around-" I glance at my watch, "-an hour's time. She looks after my fitness and nutrition business while I get to play actor and she has some things I need to sign off on."

"Later tonight then? I could cook for you. My mum is a chef you know. I have some skills," he smiles against my lips, sweetly kissing them and scrambling my brain with need.

"Arghh," I groan. "I'm on set at five in the morning, which means I have to leave around three so that the makeup girls can prettify my face."

"Tomorrow night then. If you say yes, I can wait until

then."

"Only until then?"

His breath whispers across my damp lips when he says, "If you said yes, I'd wait forever."

And there, on that bench, in that park overlooking the river, I kiss a man in public. Not just any man, a man I'm falling for so hard and so fast that if he decides not to be there when I finally hit the ground, I'll end up decimated and broken beyond repair.

# chapter 23

*Isaac*

It was a phone call with Josh that ended up being the wake-up call I needed. Well, it was more like a smack in the face, but it did the trick and had me running hard and fast towards the man I'd left broken and alone in his bed. Since the night I'd walked out of his house, he'd been the only thought in my head. No matter how hard I threw myself into work, or even my attempts at returning the flirty advances of Alice, a chef with the catering crew on location, my brain automatically returned to Flynn. If you asked me how many times I thought about him, I'd have to reply one, because he never really left my head.

"**H**ow're the kids? Are they enjoying the sand, sea and sunshine?"

I can hear waves in the background and Arty's baby babble. It makes my heart ache with yearning, wanting to be there with them.

Maybe I should go? Get the job finished here and take the first plane to the island whether Josh wants me there or not. I know Ivy and Arty would be happy to see me, I could rent a little place close by…

"They're fine. We're all fine. You don't need to worry about us."

It's almost like he's annoyed that I asked about them, like by doing something as innocent as asking if they are having fun I'm questioning his parental skills. I let that thought slide and try to keep the tone of our conversation upbeat.

"How long are you planning on staying out there?"

"Indefinitely."

"What about school?"

"What about it? The kids have years yet before they have to attend and Ibiza has schools, they can join one here."

"I didn't exclusively mean the kids. I was asking about your job."

"I'm not a teacher anymore. That's my past."

"Are you leaving everything in the past? Even us?"

Silence.

"Laura wouldn't want this for you, Josh. You loved your job. You…"

"Newsflash, Isaac. Laura isn't around to give a shit what

212

I do. I'm sick of hearing about what she would want for me. *She's. Not. Here.*"

"You're wrong. She's always here. Your kids are evidence of that."

I shouldn't provoke a reaction from him. I didn't want to bait him into another argument.

"Stop. Just fucking stop. I am not going to be lectured by a man who can't even pick a gender and stick with it. A man who has never had a serious relationship in his life. Come back and preach to me when you've lost the most precious thing you ever had. Then you can reprimand me and inform me of everything I'm doing wrong in the name of my dead wife."

He hangs up.

My steadfast, earnest and dependable brother is gone. I think the man he was died with Laura.

My phone drops from my fingertips and bounces off the bed onto the carpeted floor of my room. I bow my head and run my hands through my hair over and over until my thoughts clear.

I can't change what happened and return Josh's life to what it once was. I can only hope he finds his way back, and I'll be waiting to welcome him when he does. I have to believe this.

*I'll be waiting for him.*

*Come back and preach to me when you've lost the most precious thing you ever had.*

## one

I think I already have. Only, I have a chance to get it back.

The next day brought with it a new set of challenges. After leaving Flynn that night, I refused to work at the Cardiff location, wanting to put some distance between us.

Jake was pissed. He had a rough idea of my reasons and thought I'd pulled my usual move of fuck and run. The thing is, he's right. Only not in the way he thinks.

This had me miles away from Flynn, stuck in a field in the middle of nowhere when I needed to be back at the main location waiting for the opportunity to get Flynn alone.

Luckily, it was Jake who gave me that opportunity when he called to order me back. He was a little surprised that I didn't argue, and I didn't tell him he'd given me just what I wanted.

Finding Flynn was also easier than I thought.

He was knuckle deep in plasterboard, having just punched through a fake stud wall. I bet he pictured my face as he drew back his fist for another shot.

Getting him to meet me also came easier than I deserved but my luck ran out when he couldn't come back to my place. I was desperate to be close to him again, eager for him to claim me once more. I hoped that one day soon I'd get to sink deep into his body, but for now, I was more than willing to be the one receiving. I knew Flynn wasn't ready to take that step yet, but it didn't stop me fantasising about plunging my cock between the firm, muscled globes of his perfectly sculpted arse. I thanked the heavens daily for the long hours Flynn has spent honing his body, particularly with power squats, and I wanted to show this appreciation by worshipping every muscled inch.

My disappointment was quickly allayed when he agreed to come over tonight. After a full day on set, I'm currently on *FaceTime* with my mother while she talks me through making satay chicken on a bed of courgette noodles. When I texted this morning asking her for a low fat, low carb, high protein but more importantly a tasty meal that I could knock up in less than thirty minutes, she sent me a list of ingredients, and I grabbed everything I needed on my way home. Japanese rice wine vinegar was a little difficult to find in the local *Spar* shop, so I had to make a detour to the local supermarket, but I still got home with plenty of time to shower, change and clean up a little.

It's times like this that I wish I'd been more like Jake and paid attention when Mum was cooking. He's a demon in the kitchen; I, on the other hand, can and have burnt water.

"Once the chicken is fried off and lightly browned, take it off the heat and place it to rest on some kitchen paper."

"Done that, next."

"Have you melted the peanut butter in some hot water?"

"Can I use the kettle for that?"

"Yes, but not by placing the PB in the kettle, boil the water and pour over the butter in a jug or bowl."

I turn my face to the tablet I have propped up against

the counter, rolling my eyes as I say, "I'm not an imbecile, Mother. I know you can't put peanut butter in an electric kettle."

"You tried to boil an egg in mine once. It's not such a stretch for me to think you've gained any cooking skills since that incident."

"That was ages ago."

"Six weeks, it was six weeks ago when you called over and we weren't home to feed you."

"Tomayto, tomato. Okay, the kettle is on, what next?"

She proceeds to talk me through the mechanics of every part of this meal and for once it works, and I end up with something edible looking, that smells great.

"So who is the lucky…"

"Guy. I'm cooking for a guy, Mum. His name is Flynn."

"Friend or…"

"More than a friend."

Silence.

I'm setting the table, checking the time so that I can plate up the enormous amount of food I've just cooked and still keep it warm when I stop dead. My mother has never been speechless before.

"Nothing to say? That's a first."

"It seems it's a night of firsts," she retorts. "My first concern is that I've never known you to cook for anyone and my second is that not once have you ever admitted to being more than friends with anyone. Boy or girl. So, of course, I'm speechless. My son has found the *one*. I don't know whether to give you the safe sex talk or demand you bring him home for dinner."

"That ship has sailed, Mum. Dad gave me the whole 'wrap it before you tap it' spiel when I was fourteen and he caught me with tattered copies of both *Playboy* and *Playgirl* under my mattress."

"Oh yes, I remember us drawing straws."

I spin around with my mouth wide open in shock to stare at her face that is grinning out at me from the eight-inch screen.

"You drew straws to see who would explain the birds and the bees to your confused, bisexual teen?"

She shrugs her shoulders at me and replies, "When you've had five boys in quick succession, you can come back and tell me a better way to have handled it. Besides, I got the short straw and ended up having to sit down with Jake. Now *that* was a ridiculous conversation."

At that, I laugh. A teen Jake wasn't much different to Jake in his twenties. I swear he lost his virginity at the time most boys are still reading comics.

"Fair enough. I forgive you. Now I really have to go. Flynn should be here any minute…" The doorbell rings and before my mother can protest, I blow her a kiss and thank her for her help. Her face disappears with her mouth wide open about to speak and demand an audience with the man I just admitted is my lover.

I switch off my tablet, otherwise she'll just ring back and hide it under a pile of magazines before rushing to the front door to welcome Flynn. Swinging the door wide, I'm greeted by a sight that turns my blood molten and has my head spinning with desire.

Flynn, in a tight white t-shirt and distressed jeans.

This man could wear a bin bag and I'd be rock hard and raring to go within seconds of laying my eyes on him.

"Perfect timing." I swing the door wide and step back to let him in. My instincts scream at me to welcome him with my mouth on his, but I don't want to scare him away before he's even through my front door.

I shouldn't have worried, the second his feet pass over the threshold, and before the door is fully closed, his lips are on mine in a drugging and demanding kiss.

"I'm starving," he smiles into my mouth.

"Good thing I cooked enough to feed a small army."

"I wasn't talking about food."

I laugh lightly against his lips before gently pushing him away.

"At the risk of sounding like a typical housewife, I've been slaving over a hot stove all afternoon. So I'm going to feed you, and you're going to like it."

He steps into me and rolls his hips to show me just how much he likes something, and I don't think it's the thought of the meal that's quickly going cold.

"Oh, I'm hoping to be fed a whole lot more."

The line is cheesy and delivered with a wink. With the confidence and swagger of the old Flynn, he breaks the contact of our bodies and takes a step back before turning to walk down the hall and straight into my kitchen. The arrogant bastard prowls through my house like he owns the place and like the besotted fool I am, I follow him.

"Wow. This looks amazing. I know you said you could cook but I was expecting a takeaway, or something precooked that you were gonna try and pass off as your own." He places the lid back on the pan filled with peanut butter sauce and chicken and spins to face me. "I'm impressed."

"Yeah, well. Don't expect it to happen often. This is a peace offering."

"So you're only going to cook for me if you have something to apologise for?"

"If you're lucky."

He laughs and takes a seat at the kitchen table. "It's like being married but without the benefits."

"What benefits?"

"Conjugal rights."

I bring the food to the table and set the pans and bowls before him, motioning for him to tuck in and help himself.

"Someone planning on getting laid tonight?"

He pauses, a ladleful of chicken in sauce hovers in mid-air dripping onto his plate. Without an ounce of humour, he looks directly at me and says, "I'm planning on *being* laid tonight."

I all but slide off my seat in a puddle of shock and overwhelming desire.

*Did he just say what I think he did?*

"Yes, Iz. I know what I want, and I want it tonight. So eat

up, because as delicious as this all looks, I know it's not what's going to sate my appetite."

*Fuck.* How the hell am I supposed to sit here and eat when my brain has just melted into a puddle and caused all the blood in my body to rush to my cock?

Around a mouthful of chicken, he grins and gives me another wink.

The bastard knows exactly what he's just done to me, and he's revelling in it.

"Are you sure you cooked this? It's delicious." He remarks, shovelling another large forkful into his mouth, a dribble of thick sauce running down his chin.

"You eat like a pig. You know that? I chuckle in an attempt to gain back some control.

"No. I eat like a man who wants his main course to be over so he can get on to dessert."

And there goes the last of my control.

I place my knife and fork on the table and stand.

"You know what else I excel at?" I ask. My fingers trembling at my sides like an addict who is staring at his next fix.

He shakes his head and with another provocative grin, stuffs his face with even more food.

"Using the microwave. So put down that fucking fork, finish what's in your mouth and then meet me in the hot tub."

He drops his fork with a clang. "You have a hot tub?"

I don't answer. Instead, I step away from the table and

slowly begin to strip. When I'm down to nothing but my boxers and Flynn's face has turned from shocked to lusty, I turn and make my way across the kitchen to the outdoor patio.

The scrape of a chair against the tiled floor lets me know he's only seconds behind me. Good. He can be the one to follow me this time. All's fair in love, war and fucking.

I flip open the cover to the tub and steam billows out into the early evening air. My rationale of coming out here was to relax Flynn. He may be eager to have his cherry popped but I remember my first time as a bottom, and the experience wasn't pleasant. I don't want that for him. I want to show him that allowing me into his body is as much about his pleasure as it is mine.

By the time I've slipped my boxers off and have one leg in the warm, bubbling water, Flynn is buck naked before me leaving a trail of clothes in his wake. His erection is proud and pointing straight at me, his eyes locked on the side view of my arse.

"And there I was thinking I might have to persuade you," I tease, before slipping my other foot into the tub and sinking down to fully submerge my body in the soothing water. As the bubbles caress my chin, I turn my eyes to Flynn.

"Are you going to stand there gawping all night or are you gonna join me?" I swoosh my arms across the surface creating rippling waves.

"Join. Definitely join." His face is filled with a heavy dose of wonder with a large amount of apprehension added on top. He keeps his gaze on mine as he slips off the leather band around his wrist, carefully placing it on the seat of a garden chair. I've never seen him take it off before. It's been on his wrist since the very day we met.

He catches me looking at the discarded bracelet, and the question must be evident on my features because he answers before I have a chance to ask. "It was Clark's. It's getting old and a little worn so I try not to wear it in water."

His admission brings the night I left him into the forefront. If we have any chance of this becoming more between us, I need to explain some things before I let him take this monumental next step.

His muscled frame should make him appear bulky and ungraceful, but his movements are always fluid and beautiful to watch. The way his thigh muscles grow taut as he climbs into the tub and his abs ripple as he straightens and sinks into the water, has me salivating and thinking that maybe talking can wait until later.

*No.* We talked after sex last time and look where that got us.

"Ah, this feels good. Doing my own stunt work and fight scenes are using muscles even I didn't know I had." Once fully submerged, he leans his head back and relaxes into the warm water.

I stare at the thick cords of muscle that run down his neck and expand over his shoulders and mull over the right things to say. Flynn must be doing the same because he speaks before I have the chance to open my mouth.

"I know I told you what Clark did, but I never explained why he thought the world would be a better place without him."

His head lifts, and he glances at the one piece of his brother he has left. My eyes follow his to land on the braided leather bracelet.

"Clark was a gentle soul. He was the kind of person that would give you the shirt off his back if he thought you needed it more." We both look away from the bracelet at the same time and our eyes meet. Wanting to give him the strength to continue, I stretch out my legs, the need to touch him and to let him know I'm here more important than my next breath.

The gesture earns me a smile as he grabs my ankles and pulls my legs up into his lap. With sure fingers, he runs his hands up and down my calves. It's something I've noticed about Flynn. When he's nervous or has something important to say, he can't seem to keep still so will always find a way to use his hands. Usually, he fiddles with his leather bracelet, but as that sits a few feet away, I get the welcome attentions of his large hands on my skin.

His eyes lock on mine when he continues and says, "He was also gay. But for whatever reason he kept that hidden from us. I'm not sure why, my parents couldn't give us much growing up, but they were always very supportive and accepting. Neither one would have turned their back on him, in fact, I think they already knew judging from some things that came out after he'd passed."

"It must have hurt to find out he had such a big secret

and didn't tell you."

His eyes betray him before he can speak the words, a watery sheen dulling their deep brown gaze.

"It fucking killed me. We were best friends you know? Sure, Clark had never had a serious girlfriend, but neither had I. I was too busy with sports, and he was always making stuff. I just thought that was our thing. I never once thought he was struggling with who he was."

"We all struggle with who we are at some point in our lives, Flynn. It's human nature. The difference is when struggling with something as fundamental to you as your sexuality when you live in a world full of 'normal' makes you feel like you're wrong. That your very existence is wrong. Everyone wants more than anything to fit in, to conform, to be who they think others, particularly those they love, want them to be. I grew up with four very straight, very focused brothers. I was just lucky that my mother saw I was different before I ever did and she encouraged us to all be who we were supposed to be." I slide forward to take his hands. "That doesn't mean I didn't struggle internally. I'm not gay, and I'm not straight. I've always been turned on by the way someone makes me feel and not by the equipment they have between their legs. I'm an equal opportunity kinda guy."

He laughs at that. It's a strained laugh, but I'll take it.

"So Clark was worried about you all finding out? That's why he thought he had no other choice?" I know the statistics of young gay men who end their lives, I know the figures are too high, even in a world that has moved on and is far more tolerant of difference than it has ever been before.

"It wasn't just that. Clark had always had issues about his self-worth. He could never see what others did. He couldn't grasp that he was bright, funny and talented and just about the best person I've ever known."

His eyes leave mine to stare off into the darkness, his wistful look changing into one of barely contained fury.

"His suicide letter mentioned a man, Robert Ashworth. Clark's tech college advisor. From what we could gather, he'd confided in this man and instead of counselling my brother, he took advantage. Robert Ashworth was married with three kids. He was also bi or maybe closeted. Whatever. The fucker made Clark believe that he loved him, even fabricated this whole scenario where he'd left his wife and kids for him, just to get into his pants. For almost a year he groomed him, then for the six months before Clark died he made him believe they were in an exclusive relationship together."

*Mother fucker.*

So much of Flynn's previous confusion, hatred and anger now make perfect sense, and my heart aches for him.

Tears trickle down his cheeks, and my soul screams when his face turns back to mine. The naked anguish he wears, the guilt he feels for the way he was with me, it's as plain as day for anyone to see.

"Don't, babe. What happened between us is in the past. Ancient history never to be repeated or brought up again. I get it. I get *all* of it."

He opens his mouth to disagree, but I don't let the first

# one

sound escape. I bring my lips to his in a chaste kiss, and he sighs into my mouth at the contact. Wrapping my arms around him, I straddle his lap and pull us tight together until we are chest to chest. This isn't about sex right now, despite both of our hard cocks pressing up against each other. This is about comfort, forgiveness and acceptance.

# chapter 24

*Flynn*

I can tell you the exact moment when the embrace I shared with Isaac turned from one of solace into one of overwhelming need.

It was seconds after I acknowledged my truths and accepted his forgiveness.

The loss of Clark would always leave a gaping hole in my chest, one nothing and no-one could fill, but Isaac Fox was quickly claiming the other parts of my soul. He had crawled through the gouge that severed my heart and seeped into my blood. Having him flowing through my veins didn't make me whole, but it made me replete.

Scar tissue is the toughest skin of all, but instead of allowing mine to keep me weak, he made me see it as proof I was still alive.

"Take me to your bed." It was time. Time to give myself to him, time to submit completely to this thing between us. This consuming, healing, powerful connection that I'd felt from the very first day we'd met.

"You don't have to…"

"I know," I kiss his lips before pulling away to look deep into his eyes. "But I want to."

On unsteady legs, I rise from the water, and a thrill runs down my spine at the hunger in Isaac's gaze as he follows the path of each rivulet.

"Less looking, more action."

I extend my hand for him to take and then it's me left agog as his lean muscles glisten and shimmer under the moonlight.

"Fuck, you're hot." I can't help it. I have to tell him how fucking much he turns me on.

I swear the look on his face is as though nobody has ever said those words to him before, which I know cannot be true. Everyone and I mean *everyone* looks at Isaac Fox and appreciates what they see. I don't care if you're a man, woman, priest or nun, there is no denying this man is beyond handsome.

"What? Cat got your tongue? Have I finally made Isaac Fox blush?"

He shakes off his bewildered look and all but growls as he tugs me towards him. "Somebody is gonna get my tongue in the next few minutes, and it isn't going to be a cat."

*Hell-fucking-O.* Isaac Fox is finally out to play, and I want him to give me everything he's got.

I devour him with my mouth in a hungry, albeit brief kiss and then forcefully tug him out of the hot tub. Unconcerned about trailing water through his house, I lead him willingly back through his kitchen, down his hallway and up his stairs.

"Second door on the right," he instructs as we get to the top of the stairs.

Just before we reach our destination, I spin around and shock the shit out of him by pinning him to the wall outside. With my entire body pushed flush against his, I stare into his face and make sure he knows just how much I want what is about to happen.

"When this door opens, I don't want any more second guesses. I don't want any more concerns about whether I want this, whether I want you." To prove my point, I thrust my cock against his and he moans deeply in the back of his throat at the sensual contact. Punctuating each roll of my hips, I enunciate clearly. "I. Want. You. Inside. Me." With a last nip to his parted lips, I turn and open the door.

When he said before that his room looked just like mine, he wasn't kidding. Inside, the only furniture is a king size bed with pale blue sheets.

"I like what you've done with the place," are my last words before I spin us towards the bed and toss him onto his back. He lands and immediately tries to rise, but I'm on him in seconds. My tongue plunges into his mouth and my body writhes against his creating a friction so delicious that we are soon both leaking with the need for more.

"Need more, Iz. Need to taste you" I rasp out and with a surprising show of strength he flips me onto my back, and the air rushes from my lungs with a huff.

"No. I'll be the one to decide what it is you need. Tonight, you're mine so just lie back and enjoy the ride, because it's gonna be a wild one."

Then he's snaking down my body. His sights firmly set on my pulsing shaft. I haven't had Isaac's mouth on me for so long that I pray he doesn't torture and tease me. I want his lush lips wrapped around my cock, and I want it now.

As if he's read my mind, but more likely because his hunger for me is directing his actions, he doesn't tempt me with long licks, he dives straight in, sucking me right to the very back of his throat in one long, fast drag.

"*Fuuucckkk.*"

My hips piston upwards and my entire body quivers. Electricity arcs across my skin, and I swear his mouth is attached to a power socket. He eats me with a ferocity that has my toes curling and my hands fisting his sheets.

"Stop, Iz. Stop," I tremble out when I'm seconds away from blowing my load. I grip his hair in my hand and pry him off my cock with a sharp tug.

"I want you inside me when I come and much more of that and it isn't going to happen."

His reply is a grin. A dirty, sex-filled, salacious grin.

"Under the pillows, lube and rubbers. Reach up and get

them, babe."

My numb fingers release the cotton of his sheets, and I stretch up one hand to retrieve them. When I feel the bottle on my fingertips, I close my hand around it and slide it from its hiding place.

"Just lube. No need for rubbers. I'm clean. I got tested as part of my film contract, and I want my first time to be just you, just us. I trust you, Iz." He rises from between my legs, looking from my face to the bottle now extended towards him. With a swallow, he replies, "I've never been inside anyone bare. I'm clean too. Got tested a while back and there's been nobody else for a long time."

"You didn't fuck Céline after I left that night?" It's stupid to bring up that night long ago, but I can't help asking.

"I wasn't there for Céline. I left straight after you did. I didn't fuck her."

"Okay, then," I whisper, my voice catching with an unnamed emotion. "Just us."

I place the bottle in his hand and move to get on my hands and knees. The bottle hits the bed with a thud and his hands still my hips before I'm halfway turned.

"No. Not like that. I'm not taking you from behind the first time. I want to see your face, and I think it'd be better for you if you controlled things." He lies on his back alongside me, and I peer down at him in confusion.

"You're gonna ride me, Flynn Phillips. You're gonna take what you need exactly how you want it."

*Shine-a-fucking-light.* As my non-swearing mother

231

would say, without the effing of course. He wants me to ride his cock?

I swallow thickly and look down his straining shaft. It's long, thick and perfectly formed. I want to know how it feels inside me so badly, but did I mention how fucking long and thick it is?

"I don't think I can… I mean, I'd rather you just…"

He reaches out and runs his palm over my side from ribs to hip. "Trust me. This way will be better for you. You call the shots. You take what you want."

His soothing touch, the emotion reflected in his hazel eyes and the way he looks at me like I'm not just something to him but his everything, takes the edge off my nerves. But it's his next words that send a fucking inferno through my veins.

"So scoot up here and sit on my face. I'm going to open you up with my tongue."

*Somebody call an ambulance.* I think I'm seconds away from a cardiac arrest.

Sheer instinctual need has me obeying his orders without him having to ask me again. With a knee on either side of his head, I look into his desire filled eyes, before he scoots down further and licks me from tip to base. When his wicked tongue traces further down, and he slowly sucks my balls into his warm mouth one after the other, I swear I see stars.

Lower and lower his wet heat travels, over my sensitive and rarely touched taint until firm hands part my cheeks and warm air tickles my puckered hole which clenches in response.

Then sensation is everywhere as firm licks tease my opening, a feeling that spreads through me like wildfire and pulses through my cock which stands hard and heavy, weeping with the need for release.

Isaac points his tongue and ruthlessly thrusts it past the initial ring of resistance. The feeling foreign, dirty but oh so fucking good.

"More, Iz. Give me more."

A finger joins his tongue, at first tapping at my opening sending tingles straight to my balls. When it's slick with his saliva, he teases in the tip, his mouth still licking and sucking overpowering the slight sting I feel at the obtrusion. Slowly, so slowing he pushes it further and the sting turns into a burn before quickly fading out when he begins to pump.

In and out. Lick and suck.

Over and over and over, until I'm delirious and humping thin air, grinding my arse against his face in a wanton display of my desire.

"More."

Another finger is added and the process repeated, only now the burn intensifies as he scissors and twists and stretches me in preparation, yet my cock still throbs. The slight discomfort nothing compared to the want pulsing through my veins.

"Good, babe, so good." He mumbles beneath me. His praise like a flame to an incendiary device.

# one

I lift up and lose his tongue and fingers, his eyes immediately flicking to mine, his mouth and chin glistening with saliva.

"Need you inside me. Need it now," I pant out between ragged breaths.

With a close of his eyes and a quick nod, he pushes himself back up the bed at the same time I slink down.

With quick fingers, he uncaps the bottle of lube and thoroughly covers his cock.

"Lower yourself on me, babe. Use your hands to guide me in."

You'd think after the attention he just paid to my hole, that this would be the easy part. I'm so turned on that when I place the tip of his slick cock at my entrance, I'm frustrated he doesn't just slip in.

"Relax," he says while rubbing his hands up my taut thighs. "Bear down on me, push out and let me in."

*Easy for him to say.*

Fumbling and unsure, I did as he instructed and bore down as he lightly pushes up. When my opening finally lets in just the very tip of his cock, I have to swallow a groan of pain. Fuck me that hurts.

My previously rock hard cock begins to deflate and my face grimaces with determination to let him inside.

"Ssh, it'll get easier, don't force me. Let me in."

"I'm trying to let you…" he slips in another inch and fire floods my tight channel "…in". The noise I emit is a pained one, but he's finally inside, and I try to temper my reactions, needing him to fulfil his promise and make this good.

"Fuck, babe. You're so tight." His hips tilt up, and I continue to bear down until I am fully seated on his cock, my own length now only semi-hard and his balls flush against my arse.

I pry open my eyes and stare down at the man who is the first person I have ever let inside me, body and mind. The connection I feel to him is overwhelming.

My eyes on his, I slowly rise up an inch and then sit back down, over and over I repeat the move until the discomfort subsides and the burn turns into one of pleasure. My cock reawakens, as he gently thrusts to meet my movements, the head of his cock lightly teasing a spot inside me that has me groaning for more.

"Can you feel that, babe? You want more?"

"Yes," I exhale rolling my hips to deepen that feeling when he's fully seated inside me.

With a measured pump of his hips, the next thrust doesn't just stroke over that magical spot, it nails it, and my mouth opens on a silent scream.

"That's it, babe. Ride me harder."

My cock is as hard as a rock and bouncing painfully as I increase my movements chasing that feeling that has me ready to explode.

With my legs beginning to tremble, I rest my palms on his chest to steady myself, and then I move with purpose. He pours more lube into his hand and then wraps a tight fist around my bobbing cock at the same moment I bear down, and the dual sensations strip the air from my lungs.

"Breathe, Flynn," he whispers before claiming my lips. His hand pumps my shaft while his tongue fucks into my mouth to the same rhythm I bounce on his cock. It's too good. It's too much, and I don't have the chance to warn him I'm about to come. Tearing my lips from his, my head rears back, and I roar. My cum spills all over his hand, and thick ribbons of my release paint his chest. The sight of me coming apart all over him has him thrusting only twice more, and he punches his hips upwards gaining him yet more of my never-ending ejaculation. It patterns the perfect ridges of his taut body and with a groan to rival mine, both his hands grip my hips as he digs his cock deep one last time, and floods me with his release.

Completely spent, I collapse on top of him. His cock still twitching inside me, a delicious soreness letting me know he's still there. Still a part of me.

One. That's what we now are. Two bodies, two hearts, two souls wrapped together so tightly that where he ends, I begin.

"Don't move," he breathes out when I shiver against him, my body stripped, my scarred heart open and his for the taking.

"I wasn't planning to."

# chapter 25

*Isaac*

**F**ilming continues at a frantic pace, the summer months flashing by in a never-ending tangle of work and Flynn.

Every waking minute that we have free we spend together. Most of our nights are spent in each other's beds. Sometimes just to sleep, too tired from a long day on set, but mostly we fuck, our need for each other inextinguishable.

It's a novel feeling for me to want to be with someone more than once. My philosophy has always been that life is too short not to explore all it has to offer and everyone who offers themselves.

Until Flynn.

What it is that draws me to him is inexpressible. I've had plenty of handsome, fit, scorching hot men in my bed, and equally as many beautiful women, but none that I have connected with on the level I have with Flynn.

Maybe the sonnets written by poets are true.

Maybe his soul calls to mine. Maybe he's the other half of me, the key to my lock, the yin to my yang. Maybe, just as in life and dreams, love has no limitations or impossibilities.

It finds you. Not the other way around.

Maybe he's the one.

My one.

Because there is one thing that I know to be true. I've fallen for this man. This funny, cocky, incredibly sexy, utterly insatiable man.

And when we lie at night silent, spent and content in each other's arms, I know he feels the same way.

Now we have just two weeks left to wrap up filming. Two weeks left where I get to spend every night wrapped around the man I am going to be unable to give up. Yet, we have not talked about the future, or of what lies in store for us when the job is done.

I'm sitting alone in the screening trailer when Jake enters.

"Well, I never. He lives. I thought it was a rumour, like the one about Elvis, but here you are alive and breathing before my very eyes."

I shake my head and reply, "You saw me yesterday at the crew meeting."

"Yeah, I thought you were an apparition."

"What do you want, Jake? You only bug me when you

want something."

He drags the chair out from under the desk beside me and spins it around so he can straddle it and lean his chin on the backrest.

"I've invited Mum and Dad down for the weekend. They're staying with Emmy and me, but I wanted to throw a barbeque and thought you'd like to invite Phillips."

"His name is Flynn and is this some kind of weird peace offering for being a bastard to him that one time?"

"I wasn't a bastard."

"Were too."

"I was being his boss. I am still his boss, and I'm yours too."

I glance from the paused frame in front of me and look at my older brother.

"Thanks for the invite but I'm not sure we are at the meeting the family stage quite yet."

"Why not? Ask him. You know Mum will want to meet him, and you know she'll just show up at your place during the still of the night to try and catch a glimpse if you don't bring him around."

*True.* My mother is a law unto herself.

"Fine. I'll ask. Now are we ready for the scenes tomorrow? Are you happy with the bunker set up? I found the place at an old farm. It's a fair way out of Cardiff, but it's the perfect location for the finale."

Yeah, I'm distracting him with work talk, so sue me, and I give silent praise to the universe when it works.

"I saw the shots you took. It's exactly what I envisioned. Good job, little bro. I knew I hired you for a reason."

He stands and claps me on the shoulder before walking away. I think I'm off the hook until he turns in the doorway with a big smirk on his face and says, "I already invited Phillips. I'll see you both at my place on Sunday. No need to bring anything, except yourselves."

Then he leaves, laughing his arse off as he goes.

*Great. Just great.*

I try and fail to get back into work, envisioning how Jake's conversation might have gone with Flynn.

*'Phillips, you're coming around to my place with your new boyfriend on Sunday to meet the folks. Say yes, or I'll fire you.'*

Yeah, I bet it went somewhere along those lines. Jake can be a funny bastard at the best of times, and he'd get a real kick out of playing the boss card to make Flynn say yes to his invitation.

Sliding my phone out of my pocket I do the only thing I can, and I send Flynn a text.

**Looks like you're meeting my parents this weekend. Sorry about him railroading you. Jake just informed me of his plans and said you'd already agreed. I can make excuses for us. We don't have to go.**

I place the phone on the desk in front of me and go back to reviewing the footage. Flynn is in filming all day, so the likelihood of him reading that text anytime soon is low.

That's why when my phone buzzes just a few minutes later I'm surprised to see his reply.

> **Are you trying to get out of it for my sake or because you don't want to introduce me to your folks?**

*Both?*

I stare at his reply and decide to give him some honesty.

> **A little of both? My family can be quite... lively. Although, it'll only be my folks, J & E and their little one. And honestly, I've never taken anyone home before. You'll be a novelty for them. It's a lot of pressure.**

I wait and watch the little dots on my screen, knowing he's typing out his reply. When the little dots stop, I assume he's been called back on set. That is until my phone starts ringing with the song I've allocated to him. *Can't Keep My Hands To Myself* by *Selena Gomez*. Yeah, it's cheesy, but we both heard the *Kings of Leon* cover one night when we were lying in bed, and well, one thing led to another.

"Hey, are you taking a break or playing hooky?" I ask in greeting.

"If I said both would you grass me up to the director?"

I laugh and reply, "He's likely on his way to you right now

so I wouldn't hang around talking to me for too long. Have you been rehearsing your fight scenes?"

"Yeah, but I haven't called to discuss work. Just to say it's your decision."

"What is?"

"Whether or not you want us to go on the weekend. Jake caught me a little off-guard I'm not gonna lie, but I'm cool with going. I'd like to meet your parents. I feel like I know them already with all the stories you've told me."

I hesitate, trying to find the right words.

"Iz?"

"Yeah, I'm still here."

"If you're not ready…"

"I'm more than ready, but if we do this, we'll be seen as a couple to everyone important to me. That's a lot of pressure for both of us especially since we haven't defined what we are to each other."

"Iz?"

"Yeah?"

"I know what we are to each other."

"You do?" I can't help the way my voice lowers with my question, and I suddenly wish we were alone to have this conversation.

"Yeah, I do." His voice mimics mine and I wish I could see him. I bet he's twisting his beloved bracelet around his wrist.

"Iz?"

"Yeah?"

"Take me to meet your parents."

The rest of the day passes by in a manic blur. I get everything I need to done in record time and head out to the set to watch the day's final scenes.

I arrive on set right at the time Flynn, or should I say Grim, is about to kill a man in the goriest way. Covered in fake blood and with body parts strewn all over the floor around him, I find a corner from which to watch and proudly stare transfixed at the talented man before me. A man who has never acted before and yet when Jake calls 'Action' I see him transform in front of my very eyes. This is what he was born to do. He's effortless, enigmatic and he owns every scene he's in, even when he's not required to speak.

"Cut. That's a wrap for today. Go and get cleaned up. It looks like you've been in a massacre." Jake calls out, a broad grin on his face. This movie is going to be huge, and he knows it.

Flynn flicks the remnants of some fleshy substance off his hands, splattering it on the wall to his side. When he turns and begins to wipe the rest of it off on the side of his leg, he spots me in the corner. I say he spots me but the way he zones in on the exact place in which I stand, I know that he was aware of my presence all along.

"Hey, lover," he says when he's standing in front of me, quiet enough that anyone else won't have heard. Acting is like an aphrodisiac for Flynn. He always comes off set flooded with endorphins, and I'm the lucky guy that gets to take advantage.

"Hey, killer," I joke. It's the same greeting I give him anytime I watch him in action. Then I whisper, "I could totally bend you over and fuck you right now. Does that make me a twisted pervert?"

Since the first night he let me into his body, Flynn has bottomed quite a few times. He's also fucked me like a steam train on quite a few occasion and I get off on the fact that he's willing to switch things up between us constantly

"Well, considering how I look and the fact you're standing in a river of blood, I'd say it's at the very least borderline kinky."

"Shame. I guess I'll just have to take you home and clean you up. Can I fuck you then?"

"With a gleam in his eye and a sinful smile on his lips, he replies, "It depends,"

"On what?"

"On whether or not you do that thing with your tongue again."

He winks and takes a step back, and I laugh at his brazen request.

Flynn isn't shy with me anymore. What he wants he asks for and fuck if that isn't the hottest thing ever.

"Go and transform back into Flynn and I'll meet you at mine. If you're really lucky, I'll even cook for you afterwards."

"You mean order in?"

Yeah, he found out quite quickly that the first meal

I cooked for him was a fluke after I served him up burnt protein porridge for breakfast.

"Yeah, but I'll pay, *and* I'll order that dessert thing you liked last time."

*The one he ate off my naked body.*

"I'll be there in less than an hour." He jogs off excitedly, and I can only laugh at how easy he is to please.

When he's out of sight, I turn to leave and find Jake standing behind a camera staring at me.

"You love him, don't you."

I want to shrink back and deny his question, it's a default response for me. Deny everything. But I can't deny anything about Flynn."

"How'd you know?"

"Because you look at him the same way he looks at you."

I glance over my shoulder to look at the place where Flynn just stood before turning back to face my brother.

"Yeah," I admit. "I think I do."

"Scary shit isn't it?" He laughs before turning and walking away.

"No," I reply when he's left, and I'm the only one on set. "It's not as scary as I thought."

# chapter 26

*Flynn*

It's Sunday.

I'm in a button down shirt and smart dark wash jeans with two bunches of flowers in my hands.

"Ah, babe. Are they for me? You shouldn't have," Isaac teases when I walk through his front door.

"They aren't for you. They're for your mother and Jake's wife."

"And they are going to eat you up when you show up and give them these. Good job, babe. You're gonna earn yourself a fan club."

I roll my eyes at his retreating back and stand awkwardly in his hallway until he returns with a twelve pack of beers.

"You've catered for the females and I," he waves the booze in my face, "have catered for the blokes. Good teamwork,

246

babe."

"I also have something for CJ in my back pocket. He likes cars right?"

"Are you trying to steal my favourite uncle job?"

I chuckle, "Nope. But kids can be a tough gig. You've gotta bribe them to like you."

"True enough," he replies, grabbing his phone and keys and leading me towards the front door.

"I can't wait for you to meet Ivy and Arty," he says as he pulls open the door and steps out into the sunshine.

"Maybe we could fly out for a week and visit them once the film wraps up."

We still haven't talked about what's going to happen between us and I want him to know what we have isn't going to end just because our jobs have.

He stops abruptly and spins around to face me.

"You'd come with me to Ibiza?"

"I come with you anywhere," I say with a wink.

"Be serious for a second, Phillips." He only calls me that when he's trying to talk about something important. "Because if you are, I'll book our flights as soon as this horrendous barbeque is over."

"Book them. In fact, why don't we have a week there with your brother and his kids, then do some island hopping?"

A breath-taking smile covers his face, and he replies, "This may be the wrong time to say this when I'm about to take you into the lion's den and offer you up as a sacrificial lamb, but I'm in love with you, Flynn Phillips. Completely, crazily and absolutely in love."

*Gob. Smacked.*

We've never said those words to each other. We may have shown them with actions, and we may have made love and not fucked, but the actual words have never been spoken.

His admission, that one four letter word has stolen all of mine.

"It's okay, you don't need to say it back, and I shouldn't have caught you off guard in the middle of the street when your hands are full of flowers, but fuck, I couldn't help myself. It's the story of my life with you."

He leans in, lifting up on his tiptoes so as not to crush the flowers I have held in my arms and kisses me softly and sweetly before turning and making his way down the street to Jake's house.

I manage to get my feet to work and follow him in a daze.

Isaac Fox just admitted to being in love with me, and all I could do was stand there mute.

"Hey, Iz. Everyone's out the back, go straight through."

A tall, stunning woman a little younger than me with long caramel hair and beautiful aquamarine eyes hugs Isaac and places a soft kiss to his cheek. As soon as she spots me, she smiles and her entire face lights up. She's familiar, and I realise it's because I've seen her in magazines with Jake. She runs a high profile charity that she started from scratch and was recently awarded *Woman of the Year* in some TV awards ceremony. Emma Fox, Jake's wife.

"Hey Flynn, I'm so glad you could come. Mum is going

to eat you up."

"Your parents are here too?"

How many people am I meeting today?

Isaac laughs and steps back so Emma can hug me and I stand there, arms outstretched with a bouquet of flowers in each hand. She hugs me tight and chuckles against my chest as Isaac explains, "My mother likes collecting strays. First, she took in Harry, and I expect you'll meet him soon. Then Em here. She'll have you calling her Mum before you know it."

"Don't worry," Emma says releasing me and lightly patting me on the chest. "She's going to love you."

And there's that four letter word again. I know Isaac hears it because he locks his eyes with mine and smiles.

"Thanks, for inviting me. These are for you," I ramble, practically thrusting a bouquet in Emma's face.

This is what happens when I'm in uncomfortable situations. I ramble and lose all my social skills. Isaac thinks my little nervous quirk is hilarious.

"Thanks, you didn't have to, but I love flowers. Once upon a time, Jake would send me dozens and dozens of beautiful arrangements. Since this film started, I think he's forgotten. They're gorgeous, thank you."

"Did I just hear my name being taken in vain?" Jake appears over Isaac's shoulder, and Emma spins around to show him the bouquet in her arms.

"Flynn brought me flowers. I was just telling him how long it's been since I received any." Her smile is serene, but the glint in her eyes is teasing.

"Way to show us all up, Phillips," he grumbles, earning him a pat to the face from Iz as he steps around him and says, "It's not like he had to try too hard to do that, is it brother."

Jake just huffs, then leans forward to claim his wife's free hand.

"Do you need me to buy you flowers, Emmy? Because I'll buy you the whole bloody florists if you promise I can tease Iz about his boyfriend in front of Mum and Dad."

"Jake," she warns. "Play nice. You don't have to take Harry's place just because you haven't seen him for a few months. You're a grown up now, with a kid, remember?"

He pouts like a child and opens his mouth to protest, but she silences him with a kiss before laughing and dragging him into the house. She glances back at me over her shoulder and says, "I bet you didn't know your director was a big baby when he doesn't get his way." Then she adds, "Come on in. I'll protect you. You're safe with me."

Iz did warn me that his family was a little full on, and having not been a functioning part of mine for so long, I kind of like all the banter and teasing. It's what a family should be. Good-natured, fun and most of all accepting. And right now, I feel like I've been accepted.

*Just the folks to go.*

Feeling a little lighter, I follow them into the house and close the door behind me. Their place is twice the size of mine but has the same period features, albeit on a grander scale. As I walk down the large hallway, I notice another difference. My rented house just down the road is a place to sleep after a long day, but this place, it's a home. Family pictures decorate a low sideboard, and a toy box sits in the alcove under the stairs. Every inch has been touched by this family in some way, even though they haven't been here that long and don't plan to stay.

I want that.

Today I turn twenty-eight years old, and it's the first time I've wanted to be part of a family. I know my parents are still alive, and I'm determined to work on getting back the relationship we once had, a relationship that disintegrated in grief.

Would my parents accept my relationship with Isaac? After everything that happened with Clark, would they be happy that their previously, *committedly* straight son had found happiness with another man? My chest aches with the thought.

*Soon.* I tell myself. That's something to work out with Isaac in the near future, but not now. Today is about Isaac and his family, not me and mine.

I follow the sound of voices and laughter and emerge onto a large patio. A child's paddling pool sits on the grass, filled to the brim with inflatables, a small boy with dark hair splashes away happily in the water.

"Here he is," Isaac walks up to my side and takes my free hand in his.

"Mum, Dad, this is Flynn Phillips. Flynn, these are my parents, you already know Jake and Em, and the rugrat in the pool is Caleb James or CJ for short."

I smile nervously before walking up to the strikingly attractive older woman that I now know is Isaac and Jake's mother.

"It's lovely to meet you finally. I hope you like flowers."

She stands as I approach and wraps me in a warm hug.

"I love flowers," she speaks into my ear, giving me one last squeeze before taking the bouquet from my hand and bringing it to her nose.

"Once upon a time my husband would buy me flowers almost daily," she raises an eyebrow at the man across the table who looks a lot like Isaac and a little like Jake. "Then, when one of my boys wanted something or were trying to cover up mischief, they'd pick flowers from the garden and present them to me, hoping to buy my favour or forgiveness." She looks into my face and smiles. "It's good to receive flowers from a handsome man with no secret agenda."

I glance awkwardly to the side and find everyone quietly watching our interaction and then decide to man up and put my balls on the line.

"Oh, but I do have an agenda," I say while offering up a nervous smile.

"You do?" She smiles back at me knowingly.

Raising my voice slightly, but not before making eye contact with Isaac, I speak to Mrs Fox while looking at the man who moments again declared his love for me.

I nod, "Yes. I'm seeking permission to date your son."

She laughs lightly, a teasing glint in her eyes and replies,

"Jake? Oh, my sweet man, he's already married. I couldn't allow you to date him."

A huff of air slips past my lips at her mirth. "Isaac," I enunciate the two syllables of his name with a loud, clear voice. "I'd like permission to take him away for a few months, and then, when we come back, I'd like permission to move in with him."

Isaac's mouth gapes, opening and closing comically like a fish gasping for air.

"Well, my dear," she says cupping my cheek and encouraging me to face her. "I think, judging by the look on my son's face, you don't need my permission. He'd love to go away with you, and maybe if you ask him without an audience, he'll even agree to move in with you. God knows, his father and I have been trying to get him out of our place for years."

With that, she places a swift kiss to my cheek and sits back down next to Isaac's smiling father. I hear Isaac groan before saying, "Why can't you be like other mothers?" And then he's next to me, clasping my hand tightly in his. He doesn't say anything about what I just declared to his entire family, he just guides me to our seats, never letting go of his grip, even when we sit.

"Oh," Emma calls out abruptly as the conversations around us continue. "I picked up that thing for you, Iz. Let me go and get it from the kitchen."

Moments later she returns with a beautifully decorated birthday cake, the iced dedication surrounded by an army of tall candles. She sets the cake before me and I look down to see the words 'Happy Birthday, Killer' in royal blue icing.

"How did you? When did you...?" I stutter out, turning to look at the man at my side.

"I have my sources," Isaac replies before winking at Jake. He turns his smiling face to mine before placing a chaste kiss on my lips.

"Happy Birthday, babe. I think it's time you celebrated it again."

Emotion chokes up in my throat, and I'm unable to speak as I look back down at the cake. Around the edge of the piped icing is a circle of small anchors. This cake may be for me, but he hasn't forgotten the other important person with whom I share this day. *Clark.* The cake may not say his name, but I know it is meant for him too. A way to help me celebrate his life with happiness and not regret.

I say my thank you with my eyes and my touch, squeezing his hand so tightly that I swear I feel his bones creak. I'm unable to speak, fearful that the powerful emotions overtaking me will have me spilling out my feelings in front of his family. I can't let that happen, not out of embarrassment but because the first time I tell this amazing man I love him, I want us to be one. I want to be buried so deep inside him that he has no doubt that I belong to him and him to me.

"Blow out the candles and make a wish," Isaac whispers low enough that only I hear.

I glance back to the cake, then lift my eyes up and gaze at the people surrounding me. Each smiling face is open, everyone around this table welcoming me into their lives and their family with no expectations. They accept me and the role I have in their loved one's life. It's then, during the deep, shaky breath I take to blow out the tiny flames that I understand something for the first time. The words of Isaac's tattoo flash into my mind. Acceptance is serenity. It's happiness, it's understanding, it's faith in yourself and others. It's knowing that you can't change the past, but you can choose your future.

Acceptance is love.

# chapter 27

*Isaac*

The energy in the air on the last day of shooting is voltaic. It ripples over everything in electrifying, thrilling waves.

With roughly three hours left until dawn, we need to nail these last shots above ground before the sun burns away the darkness. The old bunker I found weeks before is concealed in the earth at our feet. I'm unable to stay and watch these scenes as it's my job to head over to the river that borders this property and prep for the very last shots.

In just a few hours' time, Feyness will be in the bag. Then final edits will begin making it perfect before its planned release early next year.

I stare wistfully at the actors taking their places, watching Flynn in character is my second most favourite thing to do. My most favourite is having him in my bed. With one last look, I turn and make my way towards the opposite end of this massive field, the grass long and undisturbed as per Jake's orders. He wants to preserve the area as much as possible, despite the large amounts of equipment we have to bring with us, he promised the landowner that by the time we finished, he wouldn't even know we'd been here.

Yeah, he doesn't like to make anything easy for himself.

When I arrive at the river bank, I run through everything with the stunt director, checking the angles for shooting and making sure that everything will translate onto film.

This is it. The end of the summer. But not the end of us.

The day we left Jake and Emma's, Flynn having been accepted fully as part of the Fox tribe, we'd gone straight back to my place, and before I dragged Flynn to my bed, I'd sat and booked our flights and accommodation for Ibiza. Then I took my man to bed and thoroughly wished him a very happy birthday with my hands, mouth and cock and in return he finally told me the words I already knew.

*"I love you, Iz."*

I still haven't informed Josh of our plans. I figured with the way he's been it'll be better just to turn up and bypass his annoyance.

Nate, my eldest brother and Liv, his long-term girlfriend, have seen Josh and the kids quite a lot. One of Nate's biggest nightclubs is on the island, and Josh and the kids have been staying at Nate's home there, so whenever Nate stays on business, they get to spend time together. Nate has reported back to the family that not a lot has changed with Josh. He's still buried under his grief and anger.

If I were a religious man, I would pray for him. Pray that he can move on with life for his sake and the kids.

Seeing Flynn, seeing how he's finally come to terms with his brother's loss, gives me hope for Josh. I just pray it doesn't take him ten years to find the peace and acceptance that Flynn has found.

"We all set?" Jake's voice calls out, and I pop my head up over the craggy side of the river bank to watch the entire cast and crew head in this direction.

Giving him the thumbs up, I almost lose my footing on the muddy ground and hear loud laughter and a few snickers. When I brace myself on my hands and knees, my camera dangles precariously around my neck a little too close to the water, and I feel a strong arm wrap around my bicep before I'm hauled up the steep slope and settled on the flat ground.

"Fancying an early morning swim?" Flynn's bloody and scarred face grins down at me. God, I love how he looks when he's filming. No, not the fake scars or the gore and blood, it's the life in his eyes that has me hardening in my shorts.

"Only if we're skinny dipping." I grin back, his obvious enthusiasm contagious and highly addictive.

"Hmm, sounds fun with a smaller audience. How about you warm the hot tub up for our last night in Cardiff?"

I don't get to answer with an affirmative because Callie, Jake's young production assistant calls out, "All principals on set."

"Go get 'em, Killer," I say, with a slap to Flynn's bicep.

He waggles his eyebrows at me before jogging away, and I get to do my second favourite thing: watch my man in action.

*L*ater that night, we celebrate by skinny dipping in the hot tub. The logistics of sex in water, especially when lube is a necessary part, are too much for Flynn and his rabid libido. Growling with frustration, he gathers me up in his strong arms as if I weigh no more than a feather and positions me bent over the small bistro table.

With nimble fingers and drugging strokes, he works me, opening me up for him, bringing me to the edge.

Then, when I'm begging for him, pleading for him to take me, he plunges himself deep inside and doesn't hold back.

Owning.

Claiming.

Marking.

Loving.

Making us one.

When he collapses on top of me, both of us replete, the small table groaning under our combined weight, he kisses his way across the tattoo on my shoulders and says, "You've given me this. You've given me everything, and now I'm going to do all I can to give you the world."

# epilogue

*Feyness Premiere, Leicester Square, London.*

### *Flynn*

Flashlights dazzle creating a blur of light. The roar of a crowd echoes into the night, the combination of both enough to have me tightly gripping the hand that holds mine, a fake smile plastered on my face.

*"Flynn, Flynn! Over here. Can you tell me why you decided to come out?"*

*"What's it like to be openly gay in a masculine industry?"*

*"Are you both getting married, planning to adopt?"*

*"Have you received any backlash from your fans?"*

The shouts and demands are deafening. Not one member of the press asks about the film, and it fucks me the hell off.

"Just smile and wave. Smile and wave." Isaac's hand in mine and his voice in my ear is the only thing making this bearable.

Ever since the paparazzi shots of us kissing on a secluded beach in the Balearics were splashed all over the papers, outing our relationship to the world, this intense and downright crazy attention was forced upon us.

A world renowned male photographer and straight fitness celebrity caught in an embrace made ripples the world over.

The LGBTQ community wanted to champion us. The press wanted to interrogate us, and we just wanted to be left alone to be us.

"This has to die down soon, right?" I whisper through a gritted smile.

"Yep. As soon as another straight celeb hooks up with someone of the same sex, or some reality TV puppet is caught snorting coke off a drag queen's fake tits, we'll be off the hook."

"I'm serious," I growl. "This is fucking ridiculous." I all but drag Isaac further down the red carpet, seeking the sanctuary of the cinema which seems a million miles away.

"I told you to deny everything and take a break for a while. This would have all been forgotten by now." He reminds me through a fake smile of his own.

*Fuck.* He looks amazing tonight. I've never seen Isaac in a Tux, and the sight is one I want to burn onto my retinas.

Throwing all common sense into the wind, I stop dead in the centre of the melee surrounding us and to the delight of the crowd, I pull him into my arms and land a scorching hot kiss on his lips.

# one

When he pulls away, confused and dazed and to the cheers and applause that surrounds us, I bend slightly and say directly into his ear, "I would never, and will never deny to *anyone,* what you are to me."

I lean back and allow him to compose himself before we continue on to the cinema. His soft fingers find the inside of my wrist and rub lightly over the tattoo there, tracing the lines over and over.

We recently got matching tattoos as a way to celebrate the purchase of our first house together. Both of us have an anchor. The only difference is that I have his initials entwined within the rope and he has mine.

Underneath my tattoo, it reads *No matter the distance* and under Isaac's it says *My home is with you.*

With the lights on our backs and our hands entwined, we walk into the darkened theatre. People think that when an actor attends a premiere, it's the first time he's seen the film that he's just spent the last few months of his life making. It's often untrue.

Last night at Jake's house, we gathered with family, friends and the all the other actors and watched the often gruesome, often horrific masterpiece we'd all played a little part in making.

It was surreal to watch myself on screen, even if the menacing man looks nothing like me, for a few months I became him, and my scars helped me portray his. For once my scars had value. For the first time in my life, I appreciated what I went through to get them.

Once the showing ended, and when everyone cheered and applauded, Jake gave a speech to thank everyone for making one of his dreams a reality. His final sentence struck me deep.

"This was possible not because of one person, but because of an army. Life is not a solitary affair. It's only magical because we get to share it with everyone else."

When I accepted my feelings for Isaac, it felt like we became one. To some extent we did, but over the last few months I've realised that loving, laughing and living come from more than just one person. They come from a family. They originate from every individual who offers you their love, and I'd willingly pay any price for that.

Love isn't one plus one.

It's one plus one plus one times infinity.

# Special Note

Losing someone you love makes you an expert on all sorts of things.

You know what it's like to will someone back to life.

If you believe in a higher power, you'll know what it's like to beg or to wager. You promise to go to church or to pray more; you'll promise to be better, to *do* better, just to get them back.

You'll feel guilty, and you'll feel selfish.

You may ask why them or why me?

But what you are not is me, and what I am not is you. I am not an expert on losing *your* loved one. I am an unfortunate expert on losing mine.

One thing I do believe, with my very soul, is that those we have lost would not wish for us to remember them with tears, but with love.

If you are reading this, this is me telling you it is okay to be sad. I am too. It's okay to cry, but never, ever forget to live.

Live for them.

But most importantly, live for you.

# Playlist

Just Like A Pill – Pink

Need You Tonight – INXS

Make It Wit Chu – Queens Of The Stone Age

Let's Get It On – Marvin Gaye

Cry To Me – Solomon Burke

Take Me To Church – Hozier

With Or Without You – U2

Say Something – A Great Big World & Christina Aguilera

Everybody Hurts – R.E.M.

If It Makes You Happy – Sheryl Crow

Hands To Myself – Kings Of Leon (Selena Gomez Cover)

Pillowtalk – Zayn

All Of Me – John Legend

# Acknowledgments

I am blessed.

I've met so many amazing people since I hit publish on my first book and without their love, support and friendship I wouldn't be where I am now.

Thank you.

To all the authors who have helped me on my writing journey, including the amazing SITLO group and Manuscript Minxes; you ladies ROCK!

Big love to my 'Southern Hemisphere Twin', the lovely KA Sterritt, who keeps me sane, listens to my crazy ramblings and always has my back.

To the crazy (in the best way!) ladies in my reader's group 'E's Elite'. All the best people are bonkers, and you lot most certainly are. Thank you for your support, your friendships and your random posts that often require me to pull out my bottle of eye bleach. (Don't you dare say it's my fault or I'll cook the goat, banish the nuns and drown the mermaids!)

An extra special mention goes to the amazing ladies in

Darlene & Dexter's Book Nook, including the lady herself. When you come across special people, you know it and these ladies are special.

HUGE thanks to my super special beta readers. Sharon #GoatQueen, Nicola #TheVirginTwin, Diane #ARCQueen, Alexandra #TeaserQueen, and Karen #LubeQueen. Your support is unending, and this book would not look the way it does without you. Thank you for your tears, your laughter, your love and your crazy notes that made me wet my knickers.

To all the blogs who took a chance on a new indie author and not only read and reviewed, but recommended, pimped and promoted me and for no other reason than they love to do so. BIG SWS for you always.

My final shout-out is for my readers.

I wouldn't be here without you. Thank you for your passion, your reviews and your support of authors, be they traditional or indie. With so many amazing books out there, I'm honoured that you've bought mine.

Bookworms will rule the world!

# About The Author

Eli Carter is a mum of three from the U.K.

She is a stay-at-home mum and a part-time advocate for families of children with special needs.

Her life is pretty manic, and she often gets asked, "How do you find the time to write?"

The answer is simple; she never sleeps, but not from lack of trying.

Reading and writing are her therapy, her solace and often the one thing that gets her through the long nights. (That and copious amounts of caffeine and sugar!)

She loves to connect with readers, so please feel free to friend/follow her on Facebook, follow her on IG and Twitter or join her reader's group, E's Elite.

Facebook: www.facebook.com/escarterauthor

IG: @escarterauthor

Twitter: @escarterauthor

Made in the USA
San Bernardino, CA
30 September 2017